LOGAN WEST
PRINTER'S DEVIL

BY **CHRISTIE MERRIMAN BREAULT**

ILLUSTRATED BY

MATTHEW ARCHAMBAULT

For my family, supportive in every way imaginable.
And in memory of my Gram, Dorothy Robb,
who taught me the value of literacy
—C. M. B.

To my wife, Melissa, and my daughter, Isabella
—M. A.

For information contact:
MONDO Publishing, 980 Avenue of the Americas, New York, NY 10018
Visit our website at http://www.mondopub.com
Printed in USA

07 08 09 10   5 4 3 2 1
ISBN 1-59336-762-7

Library of Congress Cataloging-in-Publication Data

Breault, Christie Merriman.
Logan West, printer's devil / by Christie Merriman Breault ;
illustrated by Matthew Archambault.
p. cm.
Summary: In 1874, twelve-year-old Logan West's reluctant move from St.
Louis to Kansas leads to a special new friendship, a job, and some very
important lessons about his father and himself.
ISBN 1-59336-762-7 (pbk.)
[1. Frontier and pioneer life--Kansas--Fiction. 2. Fathers and
sons--Fiction. 3. Newspapers--Fiction. 4. Literacy—Fiction. 5. Earp, Wyatt,
1848-1929--Fiction 6. Kansas--History—1837-1891—Fiction.] I. Archambault,
Matthew, ill. II. Title.
PZ7.B73932Log 2006
[Fic]--dc22

2005034185

CONTENTS

CHAPTER 1
TO SEE THE ELEPHANT

In the light of the half-moon, shadows flickered across quiet passengers as our train rambled along the Kansas prairie. The rocking motion put many travelers to sleep, and the only sound besides the metal-on-metal of the track and wheels was a fussy baby. I was about to drift off when the front door slid open and three men with guns broke into our quarters, shattering the peace.

"This is a robbery! Stay in your seats and don't nobody move or try to be no hero, or you'll be takin' your last long sleep beneath prairie sod!"

Pa shot straight up in his seat. Mama paled and grabbed Lizzie, pulling her onto her lap, but my little sister slept on. The crying baby howled as the brakes screeched against the tracks. A man's voice rose above the noise, arguing and angry. One of the robbers knocked him to the ground with his pistol. "Here's the railroad detective!" the thief mocked. "I don't reckon he'll be a problem today."

I turned to Pa, but he only adjusted his waistcoat and stared at the floor.

The robbers started at the front of the car, ordering passengers to drop valuables into their bags. Pa handed them his wallet before reaching over and sliding Mama's wedding band off her finger. "Please don't hurt us," he pleaded.

The outlaw stopped his looting and leered at him. "What kind of man are you?" His long mustache twitched when he spoke. He looked young but deadly. In one swift movement, he grabbed the collar of my jacket and hauled me to my feet. "You recognize me, kid? The name's Jesse James."

I couldn't breathe. The man turned to my father. "You gonna raise this boy like you?" He spat at Pa's feet. "Frank! Tell this yeller-belly what happened to the last weasel we encountered."

"He's pushin' up daisies," came a low reply.

A silence fell over the passengers as they watched Jesse James humiliate my pa. His sharp eyes scanned me from head to toe, and he shook his head. "Looks to me like you already been sissified. We'll learn you to be a real man. You're comin' with us." He gave me a shove.

I looked back to see Mama crying, her arms stretched out to me. Pa stayed put, hiding his face in his hands.

"Pa! Help me!" I knew the James Gang wouldn't let me live for long. Visions of a horrible death flashed through my mind as they shoved me farther and farther from my family. "Pa!"

I thrashed and turned and felt arms around me, holding me

down. Then I heard Mama's voice, far off and pleading.

"Logan. Logan, wake up!"

I was in my bed, looking up at her worried face. I threw my arms around her.

Mama clucked her tongue. "The third nightmare this month. You must stop reading those awful stories, Logan."

I fell back onto my pillow, exhausted. She was right. Just last week, I had read how Jesse James escaped with $3,000 from the Rock Island Express.

Mama shook her head, her pearl earbobs rocking back and forth. She must have been in the middle of her nightly hair brushing—her long dark hair, usually in a tight bun, fell in loose tendrils around her shoulders. She looked like an angel, her big brown eyes peering closely at me. "Does this have anything to do with our move? I know how you hate to leave Gram and Gramps."

I shrugged. Mama gave me one of her "I know better than that" looks and pulled my quilt up under my chin. Moving from our home to some cow town in Kansas would be a nightmare I wouldn't be able to wake up from, and it was all Pa's idea. He wanted to make our home in Wichita. "Our place is with your pa" was all Mama had said. Even my grandparents quietly agreed. I was the only one to argue, and Pa darn sure wasn't listening to me.

Mama leaned down and kissed my cheek, wishing me sweet dreams. When she left, I lit my oil lamp and grabbed my journal.

People say I'm the spitting image of Pa, with the same tall, lanky build, same dark hair and blue eyes. Now that I'm nearly 12, they say we even sound the same. I say that's where the similarities end. I'm nothing like him. I like to write in this journal. You won't catch Pa doing that. He's a worker, that's it. Pa likes to be moving. I like to stay put.

Now he's got a wild hair to move us all from our home here in St. Louis to a cow town. I know he's thinking I'll finally become the son he's always wanted, one who rides horses and shoots buffalo. If only he knew me.

In three days, it will be August 30, 1874, and we'll have to board the train for Wichita. In three days, we'll leave my whole world behind.

I closed the journal and blew out my lamp, pulling the covers up around my chin and squeezing my eyes shut against all the bad dreams to come.

My bedroom door creaked, and I heard shuffling across the wood floor. I opened my eyes to see Lizzie, dressed in a calico dress, her brown hair braided and tied with yellow ribbons.

"Lizzie, what are you doing?"

She stuck her chin out. "Mama told me to come fetch your writing papers and ink. She said we need it for the trip." She said *trip* like *twip*. She gathered my supplies and sashayed out of my room, swinging her dress back and forth like a bell. I rolled my eyes. Lizzie was six going on 16.

Today I was to finish chores and last-minute packing. I had

already said my goodbyes to my friends at school. Mrs. Newman, my teacher, even used my rotten luck to lecture on what she knew about Wichita. "The founders of the town named it after a local tribe called the Wichita Indians. The correct pronunciation is *Wa-chee-ta*. The Wichita Indians live in grass huts and are friendly to settlers."

I wasn't going back to school today, however. Pa had ordered me to run errands while he went to work at Mr. Rankin's blacksmith shop. "Stock the coal bin, pack your things, help your mother, and use this to buy a good pair of work gloves for yourself," he said, handing me a silver dollar. "They're thirty-five cents down at Miller's."

After breakfast, I walked to the mercantile. I pulled the heavy glass door open, and a small bell chimed above my head.

"May I help you, son?"

I turned to see a short, bald man in an apron standing behind me, his hands on his hips, his eyebrows raised. On second glance, his eyebrows only looked raised because they were so thick and wiry and he had no other hair on his head. They reminded me of two fuzzy caterpillars crossing his forehead.

"I'm here for a pair of gloves, sir."

"Well, your timing couldn't be better. We marked our gloves down this morning. What would you be needing a pair of working gloves for, young man?" he asked, the caterpillars doing push-ups on his forehead.

"I'm not sure," I mumbled. "My pa is taking us to Kansas."

"Ah, Bleeding Kansas. Well, I suppose things have calmed

down a bit, what with the war over." He grinned, showing a gold front tooth, "It might be downright civilized. Is your pa off to see the elephant?"

"Sir?"

"It's a phrase, boy. I'm wondering if he's in search of adventure in the Wild West. You know, some men get rather too close a view, if you feel my full meaning."

I shrugged, irritated with the man's questions. It wasn't any of his business, and he had a strange way of talking.

"Aha! Here we are. Now, were you interested in tan or—." His voice trailed off as the doorbell chimed and two women entered. The shopkeeper didn't even excuse himself; he simply patted the gloves before calling out, "Ladies, how may I be of service?"

I sighed and turned back to the table. The gloves fit, so I picked them up and headed toward the counter. They were on sale for twenty-five cents, so Pa would get more change than he expected.

It was hard to pass up the sugar confections, but Pa would know if I returned with a bag of candy. Then I saw a book on the counter—*Buffalo Bill, King of the Border Men* by Ned Buntline. I thumbed through the pages, and words like *Indians, John Brown,* and *trappers* jumped out at me. Buffalo Bill was Bill Cody's nickname. He scouted for the army and could speak different Indian languages.

"Are you going to buy the book or read it first?" the shopkeeper asked, his new customers satisfied.

"How much?" Pa expected sixty-five cents back. He would

probably use the extra ten-cent piece for a pound of ham or bacon.

"It's a dime novel, son. I'm sure you can manage that sum. That will be thirty-five cents for the book and the gloves." He lifted part of the counter that was on hinges and crossed behind to the cash box. He studied me for a minute and then reached down behind the counter, bringing up a canister of colorful beads. As he poured a scoopful into a small bag, he said, "No matter how civilized Kansas turns out to be, you might find trading beads to come in handy."

He winked solemnly. I imagined wild Indians stopping our train and shuddered as I took the small bag and handed him Pa's money.

"A fine bargain you made for yourself today, I must say," the man said.

Grabbing my purchases, I nodded my thanks and turned to leave. I was nearly to the door when the man called out. "Son?"

I turned back slowly.

"You wouldn't want to leave without your change, would you, boy?" he asked, holding the coins in his hand.

CHAPTER 2

A SURPRISE

I slipped in through the heavy front door of my grandparent's Victorian home. The sitting room was empty except for a tray with a steaming pot of hot tea, ready for the family's afternoon chat. Most adults felt children should be seen and not heard, but my grandparents had long included me in the grown-up talks regarding politics, new authors, and my own schooling. Soon we would be leaving my grandparents behind, along with their "tea time" discussions.

I ran smack dab into Gramps. "Logan, where have you been?" he asked, his voice booming. He adjusted the skinny glasses on his nose and ran a big hand through his thick, white hair, causing it to stand straight up on his head. "We've been holding the funniest story this week! Your mother is bringing in the shortbread this very minute."

I brushed past him. "I'll be right down, Gramps."

I took the stairs two at a time. In my bedroom, I tossed the gloves on my bed and grabbed my new book from inside my shirt. Buffalo Bill was a bona fide hero, and if this book could help me deal with Indians the way he did, it would be worth the ten cents I paid for it. Well, the ten cents Pa paid for it.

The characters on the front cover seemed horrible and savage with their pointed arrows and painted skin. They rode horses without bridles or the horseshoes that Pa worked on at the blacksmith shop. Even their ponies looked wild. I sighed and shoved the book under my pillow, knowing that it would have to wait. I buttoned my shirt back up and tramped downstairs.

"Logan!" Gramps hollered.

I grinned at Mama. Gramps was hard of hearing and didn't realize how loud he was. People usually leaned back when Gramps spoke. Gram, on the other hand, was the complete opposite, a tiny southern belle, so quiet that when she did speak, everyone leaned forward to hear her. At times it looked like people were bowing when they listened to my grandparents, constantly leaning forward, then back.

I kissed Gram, who sat with Lizzie on her lap. Gram touched my face and whispered, "How are ya, darlin'?"

"Fine, Gram."

"Fine?" Gram repeated, her blue eyes shining.

"Superior, first-rate, excellent, real dandy," I listed, trying to come up with five descriptors and falling one short. This was a family game we played. Gram disliked the word *fine*, stating that it was dull and unimaginative.

14

Mama sat in front of the tea set, pouring out a cup for each of us. She was my grandparents' only child, and they were fond of calling her Pearl, even though her real name was Mable. Gramps said that she was as rough as sand when she was little, but soon turned into his beautiful pearl.

Gramps recited *The Portent* by Herman Melville. It was about an abolitionist named John Brown, who used to live in Kansas. "John Brown fought against slavery," he lectured.

That reminded me of what the shopkeeper said about Bleeding Kansas. I entertained the group with a description of him. Lizzie laughed when I described his caterpillar eyebrows and how he flat-out ignored me when the two women entered the store. Careful not to mention the book, I remembered something and reached into my pocket.

"But he gave me a pouch of trading beads. I guess he thinks we're better off safe than sorry."

Darned if I wasn't immediately sorry I said that. Mama turned pale, and my grandparents exchanged concerned looks. Gram leaned over and patted Mama's knee. Gramps cleared his throat. "Now, Pearl, let's not borrow trouble. The boy's just full of those stories he reads."

Standing up, he held his hands up dramatically and stated, "But I've got the story of the week, and it all started with Mrs. Wigglesbottom and her pet canary."

Lizzie giggled and settled back in Gram's lap. Mama managed a weak smile, and I returned the pouch to my pocket, relieved that Gramps had changed the subject.

I smiled as Gramps flapped his arms and arched his neck,

imitating Mrs. Wigglesbottom's canary. But my smile faded as I realized that these afternoon stories were fast coming to an end.

After dinner, we all enjoyed the breeze that blew through the open windows. Mama darned socks while Gram stitched pillowcases for our new home. Gramps and Pa hunched over a chess game, and I read aloud to Lizzie.

The mantle clock chimed eight times. Gramps yawned and stood up. "Cyrus, I think I've got you on the run. Too bad I have to put these old bones to bed." He smiled broadly at Gram. "May I escort you to your room, miss?"

"Bedtime for you, too, Lizzie," Mama said.

I thought of the new book under my pillow. "I'm going, too. I feel a headache coming on."

Mama, looking concerned, immediately held her hand to my forehead. She frowned. Obviously, I wasn't running a fever. "Maybe you got overheated. Get a good night's rest."

I said goodnight and was heading up the stairs when Pa stopped me. "Logan, I trust you were able to get a decent pair of gloves?"

"Yes. Oh, I forgot. I have your change." Digging into my trousers, I produced sixty-five cents and handed it to him. I felt a real headache coming on.

Pa stared at the change. "I need you up early tomorrow; bring the gloves with you. Good night now."

"Good night."

Upstairs, I fished my book out. There was enough daylight left to read for a while. I pulled off my boots and curled up on my feather mattress. The book hooked me from the beginning. I didn't notice the room darken, and fell asleep dreaming of wild Indians. The pages of my book lay open beside me.

"Logan, wake up. Your father wants you downstairs right away." Mama jostled my shoulder. "You fell asleep reading again, didn't you?" She picked up the book. Before I could shake the sleep away, she dog-eared the page and set it on my bedside table.

"There are buttermilk biscuits on the table. He's out on the front porch, so don't keep him waiting. You'd better fetch those new gloves." She left the room.

I looked at the book. Mama hadn't noticed it was new. Maybe I was worried for nothing.

Pa was on the front porch, rubbing oil on his scuffed boots. "I need you to lend me a hand down at the shop this morning."

"You need my help?" Pa never asked me to help him.

He didn't reply; he just pulled his boots on and stepped off the porch. On our way to the stable, I couldn't let it rest. "Why are you so short-handed today?"

Pa shrugged. "Eat your biscuit."

I worked the entire day, wondering why Pa would want my help on his last day of work. Maybe he knew about the book and wanted to work the dime out of me.

At four o'clock, Pa said, "I need to see Mr. Rankin." Mr. Rankin, Pa's boss, was a difficult man. Pa never missed a day of work, not one day, but Mr. Rankin always seemed to find fault with him.

I sensed Pa would rather spit at Mr. Rankin than speak to him, but today he needed his pay for our trip. As we neared the office, Pa's shoulders hunched as he removed his hat. Pa knocked.

A voice boomed from behind the door. "Enter." Smoke hung like a thick fog inside the dark room, and it took a moment for my eyes to adjust. Mr. Rankin sat behind a large oak desk, looking disgusted. "What is it, West?"

Pa's voice was low but steady as he reminded Mr. Rankin that today was his last day and he would appreciate his pay.

Mr. Rankin studied him as he puffed his cigar. His chest heaved forward as he leaned across his desk. "You trying to order me around?"

Pa's shoulders stiffened. "I only want what's owed me," he said evenly.

I looked at Pa. He wasn't fooling. Mr. Rankin seemed to see something in Pa's stance, because he just shook his head and crossed the room to a large safe. He glanced over his shoulder before turning the combination lock. "You men always leave me high and dry," he grumbled, handing several coins to Pa.

Pa pocketed them, and we exited without another word. I looked back at Mr. Rankin's office. No wonder Pa wanted to leave this place. Outside a gust of wind blew, and I imagined it taking Pa's troubles with it. His step seemed lighter as he looked ahead.

"You did a fine day's work today, Logan. You could learn more if you tried. A boy your age should be learning a trade."

I nearly tripped. I might have learned more if he'd ever taken me with him, but here he waits until his last day! Silence followed us all the way home. Pa whistled, making me wonder what he was so cotton-pickin' happy about.

I trailed him into the house, turning to close the door. I looked in the parlor; it was empty. Where had Pa gone? Lizzie appeared in the hallway, dressed in her blue Sunday-best dress. She grabbed my hand, leading me straight past the foyer and into the dining room. The flickering candles caught my eye, and I stared blankly at a lopsided cake.

"Happy birthday!"

I had forgotten my own birthday!

"I helped Mama make your favorite cake," Lizzie said. "I tipped it out too soon. I shoulda left it in the pan."

Gramps lifted a knife. "Make a wish and blow out those candles!"

I knew the wish I really wanted would never come true. Wishes like that took more than birthday candles. I'd have better luck with a shooting star or a penny down the well. I wished for a safe trip and blew out 12 candles.

After everyone had a piece of cake, Lizzie gave me a pained look. "If I had more money, I'd a got you a bigger present."

"What do you mean, a bigger present?" I asked, lifting the tablecloth and peeking underneath.

Giggling, Lizzie removed a small box from the sideboard. Clumsily drawn butterflies decorated the brown paper. Suddenly shy, she handed me the gift.

"What could this be?" I asked, shaking it.

"Stop that!"

I opened the gift and felt a softening for my little sister, even if she was a pain sometimes. It was a book—*David Copperfield* by Charles Dickens. Lizzie could hardly contain herself, her grin showing the loss of her two front teeth. I hugged her and opened the rest of the gifts. Gram and Gramps gave me a new ink set with fine paper to use to write to them. Mama wove bookmarks from colored ribbons and used them to mark her favorite poems in a collection of Shakespeare's sonnets. I was overwhelmed.

Pa's voice interrupted. "It's my son's twelfth birthday. I was inclined to go all out." He stepped into the hallway and returned with a long, poorly wrapped gift. Handing it to me, he declared, "It was rather expensive, but if it helps us bridge a gap, then it's money well spent."

Quizzically, I tore the paper off. My hands froze in midair.

"It's a Winchester '73, Logan, a fine rifle for a boy your age. Lift it to your shoulder and get the feel of it."

The cold rifle felt heavy and awkward in my hands. Gramps commented on how fine it was. Gram also tried to be considerate of my father's pride. Lizzie was front and center, staring up at me as if I would be soldiering off at any minute and she might salute. Only Mama remained quiet. Our eyes met, and she lifted her eyebrows in silent direction.

I slid the rifle to the floor and turned to shake Pa's hand. "Thank you, sir. I...I don't know what to say."

"Take good care of it, and I'll show you how to use it when we're settled in Wichita." He turned to Mama. "Now, how about some lemonade, Mable?"

I always hated the fact that I couldn't think of the right thing

to say until ten minutes after the fact. *Pa, I don't want to hunt.* How was I to know I would be thankful for that rifle sooner than I thought?

CHAPTER 3
JOURNEY WEST

Waving goodbye to my grandparents was the hardest thing I ever had to do. Mama cried softly into her handkerchief, and Pa kept his hand on her elbow. Lizzie waved excitedly, ready for the new adventure.

As we rattled away from St. Louis, I kept my eyes fixed on the scenery outside the train window. Mama worried that Jesse James and his gang might rob us, but I assured her he was well south of us in Oklahoma Territory. I had read that Jesse James and his band of outlaws robbed the Rock Island Express. We were traveling to Wichita on the railroad.

Lizzie kicked her legs out, exclaiming, "We're going so fast!"

Pa spoke with a man who had a paper folded beneath his feet. "Whose rag is that, sir?"

"It's the *Kansas Daily Commonwealth* out of Topeka, Kansas," the man answered. "Care to read it?"

Pa thanked him and immediately handed the newspaper to me. The man smiled at this. Maybe he thought Pa was being kind. I opened the paper. The first story caught my attention.

BROKE JAIL
The Dickinson County Jail Empty

Last Sunday night, the prisoners in jail—four in number — escaped by making a hole through the stone wall under one of the windows. The "birds" are as follows: Tom Carson, awaiting trial for shooting with intent to kill; Tom Keenan, charged with horse stealing; a peddler; and another prisoner. As usual, much fuss was made about the escape, but the fleeing fugitives remain at large. The fact is our that jail is not worth a fig for the keeping of prisoners.

Great, wonderful, spectacular, top-notch. I read more about cowboys and other loose characters spending large sums of money when they were paid after their long cattle drive from Texas. Gamblers, bartenders, and other types gravitated to wherever the cowboys were so as to give them a good chance to invest their money in fun.

I put the paper down and stared back out across the countryside. Wichita would be full of these shady characters, but what about the common folk living there? Surely there were decent people like Pa and Mama wanting to start a new life. What did they think about living in a town driven by cowboys?

Out the window, the rolling hills and thick trees of Missouri fell behind us. The ground here looked hard and beaten, likely tramped down by buffalo herds. Tall bluestem grass had seeded out and offered up feathery tips to an endless blue sky. There were only a few trees scattered here and there.

This was the way to travel, fast and comfortable. Gramps had insisted we travel by train and helped Pa purchase the tickets. I closed my eyes and imagined how much slower it would be if we had come by wagon. Our wheels would feel every bump and groove of the trail. Earlier I had seen covered wagons in the distance with people walking behind them. I wondered what it would be like to walk across an entire state.

How amazing it would be to stay on this train, traveling all the way to California to see the Pacific Ocean. Why, I could turn right around and cross all the way back across this entire nation and see the Atlantic Ocean, now that the railroad was transcontinental. Of course, I'd have to hide myself in a boxcar, since I had no earthly way of paying.

That evening, Lizzie began to grumble. She had sat for hours and stretched her legs only a few times. "When are we going to be there?" she wailed. "My bottom hurts from sitting!"

Pa reached his hand across and patted her knee. "Try to sleep, Lizzie. It's the fastest way to travel."

She gave him a doubtful look but leaned her head back and closed her eyes. Two minutes later, they were open again. "I can't sleep!" Her eyes widened. "Tell me a story like Gramps does. Please, Pa!"

Pa looked up helplessly. Mama was about to speak when I interrupted. "I'll do it. I'll tell you a story, Lizzie."

Pa relaxed and Lizzie accepted this by curling her legs up under her and laying her head on Mama's lap.

Now there are a number of ways to tell a story, but I have

learned in my years that a good story should work in threes. Three ogres, three attempts to save the princess, with three different weapons of course, before the one all-important happy ending. I knew Lizzie liked stories about pretty princesses and decided to have the damsel in distress come from St. Louis where her wonderful family loved her and took care of her. Of course, wild Kansas Indians attacked.

Pa and Mama exchanged looks. Lizzie looked riveted. Ten minutes into it, I hadn't decided who was going to save the girl in my story. Then I had it. "Just then, her pa rushed out of the bushes, shot his pistol in the air, scaring the horses and causing them to tear off into the night. The Pawnee were so taken by surprise that they just stood there stunned-like."

Pa nudged me. Lizzie was snoring.

Mama smiled. "You have your grandfather's gift of storytelling, Logan."

"Thanks." For some reason, I looked at Pa.

"Maybe your damsel should solve her own problems instead of having her pa rescue her," he said, mildly.

I barely managed a "Yes, sir" without spitting. I didn't exactly see him volunteering to tell a story. Durn if he ever even tried. "I'm going to get some air," I stated, excusing myself.

I walked toward the back of the train and opened the small door that led to the platform, thankful to get away. Seemed like time away from Pa was what I most looked forward to.

CHAPTER 4

DAISY

We raced westward towards our future, and I faced east, looking back towards St. Louis, back towards Gram and Gramps, my back turned on Wichita.

The evening air cooled my nerves. The sky welcomed a pale moon, and a wide ribbon of black starlings flew overhead. I watched wave after wave of their darkening dance, listening to their scattered chittering above the clattering of the track. I had never seen so many birds in my life.

"What must their view be like?"

I turned to see a girl about my age staring up at the long swath of birds. She had a long dark braid down her back and looked like an older version of Lizzie, only her skin was a deeper tan than Mama would ever allow my sister to have.

She grinned. "Do you speak English?"

"Oh. No. I'm sorry. I mean, yes. I do speak English...uh,

obviously." My voice trailed off.

She seemed pleased with my discomfort. "My name is Daisy." She held out her hand.

I wasn't entirely certain if it was at all ladylike to introduce oneself all alone on a train. Gram would certainly not approve. But this didn't look like a girl who cared in the least.

I decided to shake her hand—it would be rude not to. "I'm Logan." I realized we were still holding hands and immediately dropped mine.

"Where are you headed?" she asked.

"Wichita."

She smiled, and I was amazed at her perfectly straight teeth. "So we'll be classmates. That is, if you go to school."

"Of course I go to school," I scoffed. What did she take me for, some sort of fool?

"This is Kiowa territory."

"How do you know that?"

"My father and I have made this trip a dozen times. He tells me all about the adventures he had before I was born, crossing this prairie with only his horse for company."

I made a mental note that she hadn't mentioned a mother. "Why did he do that?"

"He traded with Indians," she answered, fingering her necklace. "This was made by a Kiowa woman."

My mind raced with questions. "I heard only the army traded with Indians."

"Well, I guess you heard wrong," she retorted, her brown eyes glinting. "Pa made friends with the Kiowa and the Comanche.

They trusted him. He even ransomed kidnapped settlers."

"Why do they kidnap people?" I asked, thinking of the story I told Lizzie. It seemed make-believe, more fairy tale than fact.

"They raise the children as their own. Many of their natural babies die, you know." Daisy looked sorry for them. She glanced up at the moon. "The Arapaho call this the tenth moon, the Moon of Drying Grass."

I was fascinated. "I'd like to meet your pa," I said in all honesty.

Daisy studied my face for a moment before answering. "He's resting right now. I'd best be getting back. Excuse me."

"It was nice to meet you, Daisy."

She smiled warmly at me and then turned to leave. Daisy. My first acquaintance outside of Missouri, and I was sure I could see the sunset in her eyes.

I returned to see Mama sleeping peacefully, with Lizzie still snoring away in her lap. Pa was visiting with the man across the aisle. He turned his attention back to me when I sat down.

"I thought I'd come back and rest," I mumbled.

He nodded and looked away. I pulled my satchel out from under my seat and opened it. A book fell out and landed smack dab on Pa's foot. He picked it up.

"Is this new?" he asked, looking at the picture on the front.

My mouth went dry. I nodded.

He frowned. "Logan?"

My voice was barely loud enough for him to hear as I told him about the gloves and how they were ten cents less when I went to pick them up; how I figured he wouldn't be expecting extra change back anyway. "I should have asked first," I ended, lamely.

It was as if Pa were seeing me for the first time. "You knew it was wrong?" he asked.

I nodded.

"But you did it anyway?"

I couldn't look at him, so I looked over at Mama and Lizzie. I shrugged. "Sorry."

"A man doesn't apologize unless he means it, Logan," he said, handing me my book.

I could have tossed the book out the window, it meant so little to me now.

After an uncomfortable moment, Pa said, "Put that book down and rest your eyes. We still have a ways to go."

The light of dawn broke across the prairie outside our window when I opened my eyes again. Mama was fixing Lizzie's braids.

"Hello, sleepyhead!" Lizzie said. "We're almost there. Wasn't Pa right? The trip goes faster if you sleep."

I stood up to stretch. "Where is Pa?" I asked, noticing his empty seat.

"He went to the back to get some air," Mama said, tying a fresh ribbon into Lizzie's hair.

The high-pitched grinding of brakes broke through the hum of conversation as the train slowed to a stop.

"This stop, Wichita, Kansas," hollered a uniformed man. "Next stop, Dodge City. We'll be pullin' out in 20 minutes!"

Bustling voices filled the compartment. Outside, people yelled, waving to those inside the train. It looked like the whole town had come to greet us. The noise was incredible. I thought sure I heard gunfire behind the laughter and whooping.

Then I noticed a dark form crouching at the front of the car. He held a leather bag and a strong box under his arm. The chug and puff of steam muted the chattering of passengers. A man's voice rose above the crowd.

"It's not there, I tell you. My bag and box have gone missing."

Standing on tiptoe, I could just see above the crowd. The man hollering was tall and slender. Daisy stood beside him. "Daddy, all your remedies!"

"Don't let a soul off this train!" he demanded.

But it was too late. People filed out past him. Mama seemed occupied with Lizzie. I turned back to look for the man at the front of the car. He was gone. Maybe I was more tired than I thought. Had I really seen him?

"Stop!" Daisy's father yelled. The thief used the crowd as cover as he slunk down the aisle.

It all happened before I could think. I grabbed my rifle from underneath the seat and held it to my shoulder. My voice sounded strange in my ears. "Stop or I'll shoot!"

A woman screamed and grabbed her child. As people ducked down, the thief lost his cover and turned slowly to look down the barrel of my weapon. I saw him clearly for the first time. He didn't look much older than me. He was rail thin, a freckle-and-pimple-faced kid with a shock of red hair underneath his plug hat. He dropped his load and slowly raised his hands. "D-Don't shoot."

"Top-notch!" Daisy's father exclaimed. "Arrest this young man!" he demanded, pointing his finger at the boy and bending to

pick up his belongings. Daisy stared at me, dumbfounded. Mama looked like she might swoon right there.

Only after the boy was led from the train did I lower my rifle. Pa pushed his way up the aisle, his face tight with worry. "What do you think you're doing?" he whispered fiercely.

I shook my head. "I don't know. I just reacted."

"You could have been killed," Pa said, his back to Mama and Lizzie. "It's not even loaded, Logan."

I felt the blood drain from my face. What was I doing? Before I could think of an answer, Daisy and her father were standing in front of me.

"Young man, I owe you my gratitude. Turns out that scrapper is one of those Yankees that jumped jail a few days back. You're a quick thinker and very brave indeed." He held out his hand. "I'm Dr. John Kramer, and this is my daughter, Daisy."

Daisy stepped forward. "Daddy, this is the boy I told you about. She turned to me. "Logan, is it?"

"Logan West," I answered quietly. "This is my pa."

"Sir, you must be proud," Dr. Kramer said, reaching for Pa's hand and pumping it up and down.

"He surprised us," Pa admitted. "I'm Cyrus West." He summoned Mama and Lizzie and introduced the whole family.

Mama, however, forgot all form of manners and slung her arms around my neck. "Child! What in the world…," she cried, unable to finish.

"Mable, dear," Pa murmured, touching her shoulder.

Mama looked up and noticed Dr. Kramer and Daisy for the

first time. She stood and smoothed her dress, managing a weak smile.

Daisy tried to contain her own smile.

"We're just in from St. Louis," Pa said.

"Then I presume you haven't found a house as of yet?" Dr. Kramer asked. Pa nodded, gesturing for Mama to lead us off the train. Outside, I saw how small Wichita was, no more than a few dozen buildings all told. I turned my attention back to the group and noticed Pa still staring at me.

"Mr. West, I know of one or two houses that might be available," Dr. Kramer declared.

Pa thought for a moment and glanced again in my direction before agreeing and thanking Dr. Kramer.

"Not at all. It is I who am indebted," he attested—and then tipped his hat at me.

CHAPTER 5

EMPLOYMENT

September 25, 1874

Dear Gram and Gramps,

Hello from Wichita! We moved into a house after staying at the Occidental Hotel a few nights. Mama has the new house looking like home. Lizzie has her own bedroom, and I sleep in a loft above the kitchen. Pa found work with the blacksmith on the far side of Main Street, close to the train depot.

The first day here, I explored with Daisy, a girl I met on the train. She lives with her pa, Dr. Kramer. She showed me the rivers that meet together in the middle of town, the Arkansas and the Little Arkansas. They are not very wide, nothing like the Mississippi. The buildings are close together, but the streets are wide enough to drive a herd of Texas Longhorns down the middle. I am going to take your advice, Gramps, and use my best manners to go searching for employment. I think Pa hoped I would be interested in learning the ways of a blacksmith, but I want to make my own way. I know you'll understand.

I miss you both so much. Maybe it will get better with time like Mama says. I love you.

Sincerely,

Logan

I folded my letter paper and turned my attention back to class. After school, Mama came to fetch Lizzie so I could search for a job.

As I crossed the schoolyard, I heard a voice call out. "Hey kid, how 'bout a game of marbles?"

I turned to see a boy about two inches taller than me with a bag of marbles in his hand. His brown hair was ruffled and he had freckles on his nose.

"The name is Logan," I responded, "and no thanks. I'm busy."

The boy squinted at me. "Don't look busy."

"I have to find myself a job."

He let out a low whistle. "Good luck. Some of our pas can't even find work. What type of job you looking for, kid?"

A few boys started milling around behind him, waiting. This "kid" thing was beginning to irritate me, even though he probably didn't mean any disrespect. He might be bigger than me, but he couldn't be more than a year or two older, and I'd lay money on the table saying I was smarter.

I cleared my throat. "I want a respectable job, son. I'm not too particular as long as I can be proud of it."

"Son?" he repeated, a small grin spreading across his lips. "The name's Ethan. Ethan Nichols. And if ya ask me, anything that pays in cash is respectable. You open your hand and have someone put a silver dollar in it for a job well done...who cares how ya earned it?" Ethan asked. "All I'd be concerned with is how to spend it!" This brought a round of laughter from his friends.

Nodding, I said, "Well, Ethan, I can't argue with that." I looked at the other boys. "I'll see ya'll tomorrow."

"Yeah, we'll see you tomorrow, Logan," Ethan replied, dryly.

I admit I felt mighty full of myself walking into stores, asking if they needed help. I was so polite, some of the shopkeepers looked downright sorry they couldn't offer me a job. A few raised their eyebrows, impressed with my high manner of speaking. By the time I finished searching, I was a regular success at rejection. Most businesses were geared to cowboys, making it darn near impossible to find a respectable job.

As I left the Dunscomb Dry Goods & Groceries, I looked up at a storefront sign that read *The Wichita City Eagle*. I wondered what it would be like to work for a newspaper.

I took a deep breath and entered. The shop smelled like oil and ink. Two men in black aprons worked on metal plates while machinery churned out paper. I stood there, taking it all in. Past issues hung on the wall with headlines that read:

TOWN MARSHALL BAGS THREE BANDITS

TRAIN ROBBERS BOUND FOR DODGE CITY

RETURN OF THE SHERIFF
The Robbers Scatter and Hide

BULLETS IN THE AIR
Music From the Festive Revolver

I wanted to read them all. The stories were printed right here in this room. These men were responsible for collecting information and interviewing outlaws, bank tellers, train operators, sheriffs, and who knew who else! The pages were in perfect columns and seemed to invite me to read them. One read:

On Wednesday, a gust of wind removed seven dollars from the grasp of the fine silk gloves of Miss Alice Chambers as she emerged from Mr. Pope's Dry Goods Emporium. After a lively six-hour chase, participated in by most of the town's children, one dollar was recovered. We had supposed that the Kansas wind was of a less covetous order, but we see now that under some circumstances, even the wind enjoys a bit of fun at the expense of our town's wealthier citizens.

"May I help you?"

I turned to face a tall, well-groomed man in a fashionable silk hat. He peered over his spectacles at me.

"I wondered, sir, if…well, might you be hiring?" I stuttered. I didn't realize how badly I wanted this. I couldn't be rejected here.

The man's eyes narrowed. "Do you have experience?"

"Well, I read all the time, sir, and I'm a great speller. I wouldn't ask much for wages either." I threw the last part in without thinking.

"The only position I have is for a headline writer. We need a good one, someone who knows that the only way to sell a paper is to use words like *corpse* or *murder*." He looked at my reddening face. "You'd better run along, boy."

I searched for something that might impress him. "Sir, did you hear about the Yankee boy who was stopped on the train a few weeks back?"

He turned back slowly. "The one who tried to rob Dr. Kramer?"

I nodded. "I stopped him. I could tell that story for your paper."

He looked at me for a long moment. Finally, he shook his head. "Well, I guess for that we could try you out as a printer's devil for a week or so. Don't get too fired up; a printer's devil is just an apprentice. But it might be good to have young eyes in here. The name is Murdock. Come in tomorrow and learn a few things. The pay is $2.00 a week, and the first thing you'll be learning is how to push that broom around," he said, pointing to a tattered old broom in the corner. "Beyond that, you're on your own to learn. Don't be bothering my reporters or you'll be out of here before you can slick-talk anyone else, hear?"

"Yes, sir. Thank you very much, Mr. Murdock." I was ready to burst wide open as I ran outside and down the dusty planks of the boardwalk.

"Super, amazing, fantastic, brilliant, wonderful!" I yelled. I could probably come up with 20 more words to fit this mood. I was on my way to becoming a writer. At 12, I knew it was better to make your own way than to follow in the footsteps of another, even your own pa.

CHAPTER 6

THE TRADE

After school the next day, I strapped my books together and ran to the Eagle office for my first official workday. I slapped the barber's sign as I ran under it, whooping with excitement.

I stopped in front of the office and peered in through the glass windows before entering. Mr. Murdock was busy talking with two men, so I went in and grabbed the broom and started sweeping before he even had a chance to tell me. I noticed his peculiar glance, but he went on helping the men. I wasn't much of a sweep.

"You must be the new printer's devil." A man with sandy brown hair who was sitting behind a desk pointed to my broom bristles. They weren't even touching the floor. He motioned for me to come over.

"I'm Logan West, sir. Mr. Murdock hired me."

"You got experience, or are you here to learn, like all the

others?" he asked. "Can't be but 12. What's the old man thinking?" He folded his arms across his chest. When I didn't answer, he continued. "I'm Rudolph Short. I do all the crime reporting for the paper, and believe me, there is a fair amount of crime in this fair city. Notice the double *fair*?" he quipped, editing himself.

"Murdock keeps us working, not like Hutch, our old boss." Mr. Short gave a lopsided grin. "Now there was a capable writer, although he was fond of the drink and the most versatile cusser around."

He crossed his legs. "Nowadays we each set our own print. We have youngsters like you remove our words from the plates and put them away." He sniffed. "Remember one thing, young West, and your stay here might linger on past a few days."

"Yes, sir?"

Mr. Short leaned down toward my ear. "Remember to do whatever you're told and to keep your mouth shut. You just might…"

"Short, leave that lad alone!" I wheeled around to see a beefy, redheaded man waving his big fist. Mr. Short gave a slight smirk before returning to his work, ignoring me completely.

Picking up my broom, I headed across the room. The man held his large hand out to me and introduced himself. "I'm Patrick Whitney. Don't let that old rascal frighten you. He works like the devil, God bless him. Come watch me set type for this week's newspaper."

I was amazed at all the words that were crammed onto a page. There were metal blocks for every letter and gold-colored spacers stuck in between the skinny letters like "l" and "I" to hold them all tightly together. I understood how important it was to get the spelling right the first time.

"How long does it take to put this together?"

Mr. Whitney bent over the letters, concentrating. He adjusted the last words on a line and sat back, studying his work. "All in all, it takes near 40 hours on a good week's running. One of those other fine gentlemen will check for any mistakes before it heads to press. That's a Washington Hand Press, by heaven. We can print one copy every minute with that press," he boasted.

He stuck his thumbs under the straps of his apron and added, "Of course, if Mr. Murdock sees fit to rearrange things, that'll figure for a long night." He rubbed his big freckled hand through his red hair. "What did you say your name was?"

"I didn't, Mr. Whitney," I answered, apologetically. "I'm Logan West, sir."

"Welcome aboard, lad."

I couldn't help smiling. Mr. Whitney was so bubbly. It was fun to listen to his accent; the lilt of his words seemed almost musical. I thought he must be from Ireland or Scotland, but it was best to wait a few days before asking personal questions. *All the way from Europe to a town like Wichita—what must that be like?*

That Saturday, I slept in. The chilly mornings required an extra blanket, and it was hard to leave my warm bed, although it sagged in the middle. I got out and tugged on the ropes that crisscrossed underneath the mattress. How else could I sleep tight like Mama said?

I wrapped a blanket around me and looked out the loft

window. Mama was working in the corner of the garden beside our house, pulling weeds from the pumpkin patch. Pa stood beside her, coffee in hand. He motioned toward the back of the house, where he planned to build a barn for livestock.

It never seemed truly quiet here in Wichita. You could always hear music or laughter and sometimes gunfire, which made Mama pale. But this morning, all I heard was the chattering of blue jays as they argued over the breadcrumbs Mama had scattered on the ground. I dressed and went out to see my parents.

"Good morning!" Mama called.

"Good morning," I answered. "It feels nice out here."

"Hard to believe it could get much better," said Pa, exchanging a curious look with Mama.

"Hard to believe," I repeated, not understanding.

"But it just might," Pa added.

"Might what?"

"Maybe the two of you should go for a walk," Mama suggested.

"A fine suggestion," Pa nodded, tossing the rest of his coffee in the grass and handing her the cup.

Mama wiped it out with her apron. She looked up and winked at me. Mama was always winking. She could hardly stand to know secrets for long. Sometimes she was like a grown-up version of Lizzie.

So Mama had winked. At least I knew it was a secret, not just a walk. Besides, Pa didn't walk just to be walking. We started out toward Main Street. It wasn't long before he asked, "How's the new job?"

I couldn't pass up the opportunity for our family joke.

"Superior, first-rate, excellent, exceptional, tremendous." Pa shook his head and looked skyward. He gave me an expectant look.

"Mr. Murdock is teaching me to galley-proof." I bit my lip. "That means checking their spelling." When there was no reply, I rushed on. "They have ready-made stories that they put on boiler plates. Honestly, I never knew there was so much to putting a paper together!"

Pa poked a toothpick between his teeth, but I could tell he was listening. He nodded from time to time and asked how we chose which stories to write about. Soon, however, he ran out of things to ask, so I asked him about his work.

"It's mostly repair work here in Wichita. Farmers bring their equipment in and need me to hammer them straight instead of spending extra money to have new equipment shipped in by rail. Mr. Armstrong is near ready to retire. Then it could be my shop." He paused. "Now, how about that young lady-friend of yours?"

I could always talk about Daisy. "She's a wiz at school. She questions everything and wants to be an inventor."

"Fine aspiration."

The conversation dwindled, and Pa's step quickened, his gaze fixed on the road ahead. I realized we were heading to the stockyard. Pa had said that when we settled in Wichita, he would teach me to ride and shoot. I crossed my fingers behind my back, hoping to pass the stables without stopping.

Pa stopped. "Wait here." He crossed through a gate and disappeared into the barn. The earthy dankness of manure and wet dirt filled my nose. Whatever his surprise, I knew it was more for him than me. A moment later, he led a young black pony from the paddock. The look of pride on his face told me that this horse was mine.

Symbolically, Pa placed the reins in my hands. It was a shame that I felt so empty. He was giving a horse to a son who would rather write a story about "The Great Race" than sling one toe over a saddle.

"He's yours," Pa announced. "I made a fine trade yesterday— a week's pay and your grandfather's watch. Now you can learn to ride like every other boy out here."

The watch! Anger swelled in me as I thought of another man wearing it. Gramps had kept me occupied during church with it when I was little. The picture engraved on the front was of a fox and a crow. George Washington himself had displayed the same image above his fireplace at Mount Vernon. Gramps told me the watch reminded him not to crow about himself, lest a sly fox take what belonged to him. "Vanity is costly."

Pa eyed me closely. "Might be time to see why Buffalo Bill likes riding so much." He smiled then, something I rarely saw him do. That was true. Buffalo Bill did have his own horse at my age, even though he was probably a born rider. I looked at the pony again. Here was my chance to do more than just read about it. I nodded at Pa and reached out to pat the horse's nose, but he jerked his head and reared back, nearly knocking me off my feet.

"Steady." Pa grabbed the reins from me, his smile gone. "The first lesson is to never let him sense your fear. Be firm."

I already knew that. I had read it somewhere.

October 16, 1874

Dear Gram and Gramps,

Pa bought me a horse. I'm sorry to say he traded your watch for it, Gramps. I named him Pilgrim and am teaching him to come when I whistle (with the help of a bit of sugar). Yesterday I went to see him before the sun broke and found him lying on his side, sleeping. He let me sit on him while he was on his side like that and when I said, "Get up, Pilgrim!" he shot to his feet with me on his back!

When Pa rides him, Pilgrim is like a well-trained cattle horse. Pa likes to take him off in a hard gallop and race across the grasslands on the outskirts of town. I like riding Pilgrim now, although I wasn't too sure of him a few weeks ago. I'll write more later and tell you how we're getting along.

> *Love,*
> *Logan*

P.S. Sorry again about the watch!

CHAPTER 7

PA'S SECRET

After church that Sunday, Dr. Kramer invited us on a picnic. He licked his finger and held it into the air. "Looks like this might be the last of the good weather."

I laughed. The weather in Kansas changed at the drop of a hat. Just last week it was near 85 degrees, and by the weekend, we were all searching for extra blankets again.

"Might I suggest Mr. Munger's pond?" Dr. Kramer asked Pa.

"Who is he?"

Daisy answered. "Darius Munger built this town along with a man named James Mead. He staked out government land to offer up under the Homestead Law. Daddy says it allowed families to stake out claims and build homes. All they had to do was live on it for five years and pay ten dollars. After that, the land was theirs." She grinned and added, "I've only met Mr. Munger once, but I think he is seriously odd. He acts as the town's postmaster and wraps letters in a red hanky, stuffing them in his tall silk hat. I think he enjoys delivering them personally and catching up on all the latest gossip."

Mr. Munger's pond was the largest I'd seen, and Lizzie had no sooner dropped in a line than she screamed, "It's biting! It's biting!" She dropped the stick and ran in the opposite direction. Luckily, Daisy was close enough to grab it and yanked hard, snagging the fish.

Dr. Kramer scooped Lizzie up as she ran past. "Lizzie, look there at Daisy. You caught a fish."

Lizzie was not impressed. She remained in the doctor's arms, her head on his shoulder. I rolled my eyes and walked over to Daisy.

"It's not too small, is it?" she asked.

I shook my head and looked back at Lizzie. "Maybe it was just a little fast."

We baited more lines and threw them in. Mama spread out a quilt and poked around her picnic basket, making sure our food had traveled well. She showed Lizzie how to make a daisy-chain necklace. Dr. Kramer and Pa took opposite sides of the pond and tried their luck fishing.

An hour later, Pa had four healthy-sized bass. Daisy and I kept our fish on the same cord and pulled it up to show Mama. Lizzie peeked from behind Mama's skirt.

"My, my, we'll have quite the fish fry tonight!" Mama exclaimed, her face cheery.

I glanced over at Dr. Kramer. The corners of his mouth were

drawn, and he was muttering under his breath. He had not pulled in one fish. "Dr. Kramer! How are you faring?" I called.

He removed his hat and wiped his forehead with his white handkerchief before waving it in the air like the white flags the army used to signal surrender. "These fish and I are coming to an understanding!"

After enjoying Mama's fried chicken, Daisy and I took Lizzie on a nature walk. We collected grasses, rocks—and flowers for Mama.

Daisy showed me a small piece of limestone with an imprint of a shell on the bottom side. "I love collecting these," she said, slipping it into her pocket. "It feels like I have a link to the past— a chance to touch history."

I smiled at that. Daisy seemed to put a lot of thought into everything around her.

Bending down, I snapped a dandelion off its stem. "Look Lizzie," I said, holding it under my chin. "If there's a yellow shadow, it means I like butter."

Lizzie leaned in to peer at my chin. "You do! You do like butter. Me next!" She stared down her nose as I tickled her chin with the yellow weed.

"Yep, you're a butter lover," I proclaimed, tossing the dandelion into the tall prairie grass.

Lizzie sang a song Mama had taught her while churning butter:

Come butter come! Come butter come!
Johnny's at the garden gate
Waiting for his butter cake!
Come butter come!

Daisy was ahead of us. She returned with a tiny snake in her hands but stopped before she reached us.

"Lizzie, don't get spooked, okay?" Daisy said. "It's a baby snake, and there are more over there in the sand. Baby snakes don't bite, but they're hard to hold on to." She let the snake wind through her fingers.

"A baby snake." Lizzie crept up slowly.

"It's a bull snake," Daisy commented, pointing to its pattern. "Do you want to hold it?"

Lizzie shook her braids back and forth. "Not today."

"Maybe another day," Daisy agreed, holding it up higher. She looked at me. "How about you?"

"Sure, I've never held a snake."

I watched as the snake curled around my fingers, trying to slither away. "Want to show the others?"

We went back to share our treasures, Lizzie's chubby fists full of wildflowers.

Mama blanched when she saw what was wiggling around my fingers. "Lizzie dear, look at your beautiful collection! Let's line them up on the blanket," she said, ignoring the snake completely.

"Son of a gun," Pa exclaimed, reaching out his hands to hold our little creature.

"There's a whole mess of them in the sandbank," Daisy pointed out.

Dr. Kramer pulled a book from his bag. "I carry a couple of guidebooks with me so I can accurately identify different species."

He handed a snake identification booklet to Daisy and me. "Lizzie, why don't you have your pa help you read about the flowers you've picked?"

My head jerked up, and Mama looked down at her hands. Lizzie took the book to Pa and sat in his lap. Pa opened it and slowly flipped through a few pages. My throat was so dry, I couldn't swallow. Daisy noticed my peculiar look and stopped reading. Everyone grew quiet. Even Dr. Kramer looked bewildered.

Finally, Pa cleared his throat and closed the book, handing it back to Dr. Kramer. "I would be obliged if you could help Lizzie, John."

A look of understanding passed over Dr. Kramer's face. "Of course, I should have suggested that myself. Lizzie, why don't you bring your favorite wildflower here?"

My cheeks burned, and I felt Daisy's eyes on me. I got to my feet and took off toward the sandbank. She called after me, but I didn't wait. Tears stung my eyes, and I'd be danged if I let Daisy see my shame. At the sandbank, I fell to my knees, digging for more bull snakes.

Daisy came huffing up beside me, and I saw the tips of her brown boots nudging the sand. Her voice was soft. "Logan, it's nothing to be ashamed of. Lots of people can't read. They're better at other things, that's all. If your pa can't read, he certainly makes up for it with his skill as a blacksmith."

When I did not reply, she added quietly, "Maybe if you both found out what the other is good at, you could share it with each other."

I finally looked up at her.

"That's just it," I said evenly. "I'm good at reading."

CHAPTER 8
THE NEW PEACEKEEPER

Daisy never mentioned Pa's secret to anyone. It was as if she'd just plumb forgotten. Pa acted like nothing happened. I reckon he was used to the shame. Yet I couldn't stand that someone outside our family knew. Working helped keep my mind off of it.

I rehearsed how to ask Mr. Murdock about a story I wanted to write. Outside the shop, I saw him and Mr. Short talking to a man with a long mustache. The stranger wore a black waistcoat with a bandanna around his neck. His belt was chock full of bullets ready to slide into the two pistols that hung at his side. Most menfolk in Wichita had a pistol, and many of them kept their Peacemakers from the war, but few wore them around town. A man carrying two revolvers meant to burn powder.

Mr. Short seemed excited about this man and eagerly questioned him. I only heard bits and pieces, but it sounded as if

Mr. Short knew him already.

"We're just a short cry from Dodge," I heard him say.

The man stood tall and kept a straight face. He shook hands with both men, turned heel, and walked away. Watching him make his way down Douglas Street, I thought about his guns. He must be important. I decided to find out about him.

Inside, Mr. Short was behind his desk, scribbling furiously. I hesitated. He wasn't the type who took a shine to interruption.

"Mr. Short?"

"What!" he asked sharply.

"If you're busy…"

"I'm always busy!" He looked back down at his work and then shook his head, a smile forming. "It's just been a while since I was excited about that fact!"

"Sir?"

"Guess who's come to Wichita, young West." he said.

I stepped up to his desk. "The man outside? Who was he?"

"That's Wyatt Earp, our new assistant deputy. He's a fantastic shot, although rumor has it he prefers to use his fists. Just knowing that man is in town will likely deter some lawlessness." Mr. Short hesitated as if a thought had just occurred to him. "I suppose that means my work could slow down a bit."

He went back to scribbling notes. I decided to go to Mr. Murdock's office, where I informed him of a story I had heard at school.

"There's a kid at school named Joshua Gunn who caught a 52-pound catfish last Saturday," I reported. Mr. Murdock didn't look up. "In fact, he and his two friends caught 500 pounds of fish that day."

"Fine, fine," Mr. Murdock said, absentmindedly. "Give me 200 words for one-half cent a word. Just get a draft to me day after tomorrow." He slapped his hand on his desk to indicate our conversation was over.

I nearly skipped out of the room. My math wasn't as good as my letters, but I figured to make a whole dollar if I got this right.

Grinning, I walked past the reading room where newspapers from all parts of the country were out for the people of Wichita to come in and read. The room was not really a room at all, just an area sectioned off by low railing.

Pa sat at the table, the papers neatly folded in front of him. I swung the door to the railing open. "What are *you* doing here?"

He raised his eyebrows at my rudeness.

"I mean, is something wrong?"

He shook his head. "No, Logan, nothing's wrong. I passed by and thought I'd come see where you worked. Maybe I should have warned you."

"Logan, is this your pa?" Mr. Murdock had walked up behind me.

Pa stared at me, his blue eyes sharp. I glanced at the unopened papers. "Yes, sir, this is my pa, Cyrus West."

Mr. Murdock shook Pa's hand. "Pleasure to meet you. Logan secured his first story today. I'm sure he'll be telling you all about it."

When Pa didn't comment, Mr. Murdock pointed to the paper.

"If it's well-written, we'll run it under this section."

Pa looked at the paper. "I see."

Mr. Murdock looked from me to Pa and then back at the paper. "Well, at any rate, it was nice to meet you."

Pa nodded again but remained silent. What was he doing here? And why, of all places, was he in the reading room?

Outside, Pa answered my question. "I heard they had copies of the *St. Louis Dispatch*. I hoped to find someone reading the paper who wouldn't mind talking about it."

I frowned. Pa liked to talk with people while they read the paper; it was one of his tricks. He kept himself up on the news by acting as if he had already read an article and by asking what the other person thought. "Now what was it they said again?" he'd ask, prompting the other man to read aloud. People never caught on. Pa had been doing this long enough to pull the wool over most people's eyes.

He pulled a letter out of his shirt pocket. "This came for you."

The envelope was from Gramps. My name was above Pa's on the front with *Wichita, Kansas* underneath it. In the right-hand corner was a one-cent stamp. Pa must have recognized Gramps' handwriting and wondered if something had happened in St. Louis.

I tore open the letter, throwing a sidelong glance at Pa. He was worried; I could tell. I read the letter aloud.

October 26, 1874

Dear Logan,

Thanks for your fine letter. Gram and I look forward to your descriptions of the Wild West. How wonderful it is to hear you have your own horse. Pilgrim is a stupendous name.

As you know, we old folks are slowing down a bit. We hired help with the house, a young widow and her small son. They are Mrs. John Bradley and her boy, John Jr., age seven. To be honest, we hired her partly for the service of having help with the numerous chores this big old house requires, and partly to fill the quiet spaces. In trade, we allow them the two rooms upstairs and a small sum. I do have trouble remembering to call the boy John and not Logan, however!

You mentioned a friend in your last letter. Daisy. Now, there's a name! Gram requests a full description. Of course, she would not want to pry, would she? Now, Logan, don't forget to say your prayers and mind your parents. Please give that rascal sister of yours a hug.

All our love,
Gramps & Gram

P.S. Don't think twice about the watch. Your pa made a fine trade.

I read the last part to myself before folding the letter and stuffing it back in the envelope. The tightness in Pa's face relaxed. I reckon if something happened to Gramps or Gram, he'd feel responsible for taking us away.

We walked home without another word, lost in our own

thoughts. Coming to Wichita had a bright side. Sometimes I rode Pilgrim outside of town along the riverbank. I tucked one of my books in my saddlebag and read while he grazed on the tall prairie grass.

Daisy was usually around when I walked home after work. She had a habit of starting our conversations with a question, as if she had been wondering about something all day and couldn't wait to ask me. I knew Daisy would be important when she grew up.

And now I had my first story. It was only about a kid who caught a mess of fish, but it was a start. I never would have guessed I'd have so many things working out for me here in Wichita.

I was about to learn that luck could change on me as quick as the Kansas weather.

CHAPTER 9

LOGAN'S FIRST STORY

When I interviewed Joshua Gunn the next day, it amazed me how humble he was about his fishing skills.

"Is this really going to be in the paper?" he asked, his hands deep in his pockets. "I've never been in the paper before."

I've never written anything that's been in the paper before. I decided not to let Joshua in on that secret. "That was a darn big catfish! What bait did you use? Did it feed your entire family? Were you able to fish it out all by yourself?"

I looked down at my notes of Joshua's replies. *Worms. Yes. Yes.* His answers were not going to sell many newspapers. I wanted to fill the story with a few sensational words of my own. This had to be a good read.

"Could you elaborate?"

Joshua stared at my paper. His face colored, and he shook his head. I sighed. Interviewing was tougher than I had thought. I stuffed my notes into my pocket. "How about you show me where you caught that fish?"

Joshua brightened. We ran to the riverbank, and I spent the next half hour chatting, hoping Joshua would come out of his shell. He pulled a small brass box from his pocket. "I always use this when I'm fishin'," he said quietly. I leaned in as he lifted the lid. There was a small coil of string, three sharp hooks, three lead sinkers, and a cork for a bobber.

"What a handy fishing case!"

Joshua grinned. He told his story while I took mental notes. I wanted to write a great story, so when he used words like *big* and *dark,* I substituted them with *monstrous* and *murky.*

After I thanked him and shook his hand like a real reporter, I walked home, deep in thought. How would this story begin? Maybe I could say that we should all be grateful the good Lord did not make us a catfish on Saturday. I shook my head, trying to erase that idea.

"That's a mighty big frown!" Dr. Kramer called from his rocking chair. I crossed his yard and sat in the other chair when he offered.

"My first big story," I explained, feeling important. "I'm trying to put my thoughts in order."

He puffed on his pipe. "Well, how do you like that? Our fine paper is training a new reporter! I say, do you have experience with letters?"

I grinned. That's exactly how Ben Franklin described his love for reading and writing. I read how he decided to become a man of letters, tramping part way to Philadelphia, searching for his fortune.

"Not much experience, Dr. Kramer. Back home in St. Louis, I won first place in a writing contest at school," I explained. "But this is different. Mr. Murdock is going to pay me. That is, if it warrants being paid for." My voice trailed off.

"I find it most helpful to shut out the world when I work on my journal."

I thought of Dr. Kramer writing in a journal like Mama and I did. I didn't record an entry every day like Mama, just important things I wanted to remember, like stopping the thief on the train. It never occurred to me that Dr. Kramer wrote his own version of that day. If only Pa could be more like Dr. Kramer.

"I thought I heard you talking with someone out here." Daisy stood at the door. "Reba baked cookies. Can I interest the two of you?"

Reba had been the Kramer's housekeeper ever since Daisy's mother died from pneumonia. Reba tried her best to be a mama for Daisy, but she acted too old and grouchy. I once heard her yelling at Dr. Kramer that she would slap him to sleep if she caught him testing the cookie dough again.

We followed Daisy inside. The front room had chairs for people who needed to see Dr. Kramer. They were empty today.

An eye chart on the wall looked like the one in our doctor's office back in St. Louis. Another chart hung beside it, similar to the first one, except there was only the letter *E*—turned upside down, flipped backwards, and on its side.

Dr. Kramer spoke up. "That's for my clients who can't read.

The regular chart wouldn't be very helpful to diagnose whether or not they need spectacles if they can't read the letters in the first place. This way, they can point in the direction the 'E' is pointing," he explained. Dr. Kramer looked so directly at me, I thought he was checking my vision. "There are plenty of folks who can't read, you know." I figured he must be right if they actually made a chart like that.

Daisy appeared with a small tray of cookies. "Did you get your story?"

Relieved to have a new topic, I explained the trouble I had with Joshua but how he finally loosened up. "Now I'm trying to figure out how to begin."

"I'm sure it will come to you," Daisy assured me. I was happy she wasn't trying to offer advice. I wanted the story to be in my own words.

After a short visit, I made my way home, still turning the story over in my head. Darkness had settled in, but Pa was still working on the barn.

"Hi, Pa."

He stopped his hammer in midair and turned to me. His face was sweaty, even in the chilly night air, and he dragged his shirtsleeve over his forehead. "Whew, I reckon I'd better give this up for the evening." He took a long drink from his canteen. Noticing my paper, he asked, "What's that?"

I relayed the events of my day, deciding to skip the part about the eye chart. He listened quietly, and when I finished, he only nodded. It amazed me how Pa could make a person feel like a jabbermouth. Sort of like Joshua Gunn until I got him warmed up.

Mr. Short said everyone tends to want to talk about himself if given the chance. I glanced at the barn.

"The barn is coming along," I said. Pa had the framing nearly finished. "Sorry I haven't been much help. What will you do next?"

Pa took another long drink before answering. "I made a trade on some lumber this week. There are used nails at the shop that I'll fire and hammer back to new. Cheaper than store-bought."

"There's a burned-down farm just north of Wichita. I can run by with Pilgrim tomorrow, maybe find some more nails," I offered.

Pa blinked. "I'd appreciate that, Logan." He stood up and stretched. "But for now, I want you to work on that story your boss is expecting." He hesitated and then added, "Your grandpa would be proud."

I spent hours at the kitchen table that night, grinding out as good a story as I could muster. The light of the kerosene lamp cast shadows over my paper, and I noticed how many words I had crossed through. I wondered if the words came this hard for Mr. Murdock. I slept hard that night, dreaming of selling papers with my own headlines blazoned across the top.

CHAPTER 10
MISTAKES

I gathered nails the next afternoon. I had no problem finding the charred building, but locating the nails was a tougher chore. I thought of how awful it must have been for the settlers to have a fire destroy everything they'd worked for. There must be dozens of hard-luck stories around a town like Wichita—not something good people would want printed in the paper, though. After an hour of digging through the ashes, I had 30 nails.

I rode Pilgrim back to town and tied him to the hitching post in front of the Eagle before going in. I was learning how to lock the metal letters into type forms, being especially careful to mind my p's and q's. Since we arranged every word backwards and from right to left, it was easy to put those two particular letters in the wrong way. Mr. Murdock started the printing of each paper on the Washington Hand Press; it was his ritual. He studied the first printing before having one of the other men finish the job.

"Let's get this completed, gentlemen," Mr. Murdock hollered over the slapping of the press. "I've got handbills to print yet."

We all worked hard. Mr. Short was the quiet sort and seemed to prefer working alone. Mr. Whitney, on the other hand, finally answered some of my questions while we worked.

"Ireland is my mother country. My parents wanted to make a try for it here in America. We were a poor lot, always begging for food. They told us in the old country that there was free land here, so we took off on the next boat," Mr. Whitney explained. "The luck of the Irish wasn't to be had, however. My parents settled in New York and worked in factories for the rest of their lives. It's my plan to realize their dreams."

"Have you ever gone back to Ireland?" I asked, thinking how far it was from Wichita.

"No," he answered quietly. "I said goodbye to my grandparents and cousins." Mr. Whitney glanced up. "Look at the clock, lad. You best run along."

The clock read nine o'clock. How had it become so late? Waving goodbye, I grabbed my bag and ran outside to get Pilgrim. It was raining good and hard, and the post I'd tied Pilgrim to was empty. Pilgrim was gone!

I ran down the street yelling for him. The metallic smell of rain filled the pitch-black air, and only when lightning struck was I able to search the street.

Finally, I made my way home, imagining Pa's face when I told him I had lost Pilgrim.

"Logan!" Mama cried when she saw me. "What are you doing out in this?"

Pa walked into the room and stared at me, waiting for an answer.

"I didn't...I didn't know it was storming," I stammered. "We were working and didn't hear the rain. Pilgrim ran off."

Pa didn't miss a beat. He grabbed his coat from the wall peg and pulled his boots on. "Couldn't have gone far; ponies don't like to run in this; he's likely under a tree."

"I'll go, too," I said.

"No, boy," Pa answered sharply. "Stay here with your mama."

I looked at him helplessly. It was my horse and my mistake. "Please?" I whispered.

Mama put her hand on Pa's shoulder. He drew in a deep breath before nodding. "Grab your coat."

We searched as the storm blew harder and soaked us both but good. Lightning bolts crawled across the sky like veins under skin, snaking their way as far as they could reach before touching off another cloud. The electricity in the air raised the hair on the back of my neck.

But there was no sign of Pilgrim. We split up, and Pa walked the riverbank while I ran back to the stables. Maybe some good citizen had found Pilgrim and put him in the nearest stall. There were horses underneath two trees inside the corral. Pa was right; they didn't want to be out in this.

Pilgrim wasn't there. Thunder clapped overhead, and the horses stamped the ground. I felt hot tears prick my eyes. Lightning flashed, and I looked up to see Pa's tall figure. I felt my whole body jump and bit down on my tongue.

Rain poured off his hat. I couldn't see his face, but his voice was full of concern. "Run home and get in bed, son. I'll keep looking."

I was bone tired, so I didn't argue. The cold rain didn't let up at all during the night. I fell asleep watching the storm from the safety of my warm bed, praying Pa would bring Pilgrim home.

That's exactly what he did. When I woke the next morning, Pa was at the breakfast table. "Pilgrim was behind the train depot. I heard a whinnying after a train came in around midnight. He was near the tracks when I found him." Pa didn't have to say it; we were lucky Pilgrim hadn't been standing directly on those tracks.

"You need to double-check the knot," he said simply and changed the topic, finishing his coffee.

I ran to see Pilgrim. He was lying in the mud, taking long measured breaths. He looked as tired as I felt.

"Hey, boy," I murmured, approaching him. "Were you scared?" He sniffed at my hand, then drew in a deep breath and let it out noisily. I fished an apple out of my lunch pail. The sight of this was enough for him to sit up, although he refused to get to his feet. I fed him the apple with my open palm. Crunching it slowly, he watched me with his soft brown eyes. I wondered what would have happened to Pilgrim if he had wandered off too far.

Wichita Indians lived a few miles upriver, but they were restricted to their reservation. Pilgrim could have been roped in with their other ponies. Then again, Pilgrim might have just wandered the Kansas plains. I stroked his mane and realized how lucky I was Pa found him. Pa had shown me how to make slipknots. Hadn't I used one yesterday when I tied him up? I couldn't recall.

"I have to get to school, Pilgrim." I stroked his muzzle. "Sorry for last night." I made sure to close the gate securely.

At lunch I read the first draft of my story to Joshua to see if he might want to contribute more. Sometimes hearing a retelling of an event will jar a person's memory. Joshua, however, only smiled and said, "You make me sound real good."

I smiled too, happy he liked it. I was about to tell him so when he said, "But the catfish weren't that hard to catch, and I can't rightly recall saying what you have me saying in that story."

I swallowed. "Well, I had to straighten out your vocabulary a bit, Joshua."

"Oh."

"We have to make sure our readers get a clear picture." I stood up. "Now, I'm not sure when they'll run this story, so don't tell everyone yet, okay?"

"Okay."

Daisy giggled and peeked from behind a tree. She must have been standing there the entire time.

"Knock it off, Daisy. You shouldn't be eavesdropping."

"Oh, I was merely listening to the great-big-fish story."

I didn't smile. Something about having Daisy assessing my story bugged me. I walked away.

"Logan, wait." When I didn't respond, she grabbed my elbow. "Don't you want to know what I think?"

"Not really."

She stepped in front of me, forcing me to stop. "Listen, I'm sorry. Let's forget it, okay?"

"Fine," I agreed. We walked back into the schoolhouse and sat at our desks. I put my story away and decided to wait for a true writer to look at it. More than once that afternoon, I caught Daisy staring at me. As soon as Miss Peck dismissed us, I bolted out the door before Daisy could stop me. I raced to the *Eagle* and ran smack into Mr. Whitney.

"Whoa, laddie, slow down there." He looked behind me. "Where's that pretty girl you have a shine for?"

I made a face, and he laughed, saying something about Cupid's arrow. "Now what has you charging in here like a mad little leprechaun?" he asked, his accent bouncing every word.

I was glad to be among other writers who understood me. I pulled my notes from my bag. "It's my first story. I interviewed a boy at school about his amazing catch while fishing last weekend."

Mr. Whitney whistled and clapped me on the shoulder. "The first story is a great milestone, Logan. Good luck, lad."

My palms felt damp when I knocked at Mr. Murdock's door. "Enter."

As I walked into his office, I wondered if I should even bother him with a rough draft. Maybe he only wanted to see a finished paper. I stood at the door.

Mr. Murdock looked up over his spectacles. "Well?"

"I have a rough draft of the story you…"

"What story?"

I shifted my feet. *What did he mean what story?* "Joshua Gunn, sir."

"Who?"

"The third grader who caught the 52-pound catfish," I said, my words rushing together.

Not one sign of recognition passed over his face. He gestured for me to approach him, reaching for the paper. I handed it to him, my hands shaking.

He adjusted his glasses and read my story. There isn't a whole lot that makes me uncomfortable, but I admit that standing there watching him read what I spent hours writing just about made me pass out. Every time he frowned or narrowed his eyes or wrinkled his nose, I felt my stomach drop. What was I doing here? He would read that story and realize he should never have hired me in the first place. I wondered what it felt like to be fired.

He took off his spectacles and drummed his fingers on his desk as we stared at each other. "Logan, you've fallen into a trap that many beginning journalists find themselves unable to avoid," he commented blandly.

"Excuse me?"

"We can't print this," he said, pushing the paper toward me. "You've added a bit too much salt and pepper here, kid."

Salt and pepper? "I don't understand, Mr. Murdock."

"Look, it's not easy avoiding the urge to spice things up a bit. I spoke with this young man last night. I had to make sure we were printing reality." He glanced at the paper. "I think the true story is good enough not to be sensationalized." He circled words as he barked them out. "*Monstrous, thrashed violently, sacrificed.* Seriously, kid, you make it sound almost biblical. Tone it down. Why don't you go home and try again. The floors are swept and we can handle things here."

I swallowed hard as I made my way to the door, willing myself not to cry. Crumpling my paper, I vowed I would never set foot in the shop again. Never. I pushed my chin up and walked out the door.

"Logan, wait a minute!" Daisy called.

I groaned. Couldn't I just be alone? I turned to see her racing toward me. What was she doing here?

"Aren't you going to work?" she gasped, catching her breath.

"No."

She looked confused. "Why not?"

Good Lord, did I have to tell her everything? "I'm just not!" I snapped.

"Logan," she started, but I interrupted her.

"Why are you always hanging around? Don't you have any girlfriends? I haven't spent one day in this miserable town without you asking stupid questions nobody wants to hear. Why do you do that? Do you just like the sound of your own voice? And why are you running? Hasn't anyone ever told you how to act like a lady?"

Daisy's jaw dropped, and tears flooded her eyes. She turned and ran as fast as she could, dropping her lunch pail and books and racing down Douglas toward the river. I let her go. What could I possibly say now?

CHAPTER 11
WYATT'S ADVICE

I bent to pick up Daisy's books and scanned the people in the street. Nobody seemed to be paying me much mind. Then I saw the new deputy sitting in a wicker rocker in front of city hall. He was watching my every move. Normally, I would have walked away. But today I was feeling a little tougher in my skin. I crossed the street.

"Mr. Earp?"

"Call me Wyatt. I don't believe we've been properly introduced."

I was a bit startled; his reputation certainly didn't include good manners. I offered my hand. "I'm Logan West. I work at the newspaper."

He nodded slowly as if processing this. I watched him flick a coin between and around his knuckles on his left hand, his fingers working on their own accord. He didn't seem to be conscious of his own habit. "You a writer?"

Any other day, I might have answered differently, but today I said, "No, sir, I work as a printer's devil." I pushed the image of Daisy's tear-filled eyes out of my head.

"Too bad," Wyatt replied.

"What's too bad?"

"Well, I've taken a position here in Wichita. I figure this town has reporters that like to rub elbows with the sheriff to get a lead story. Lawmen don't take kindly to having an extra pair of eyes looking over their shoulder, taking notes. I'm no exception. I find it easiest to pick the reporter who will accompany me if I have to ride after a troublemaker."

"I didn't know reporters went along."

"They go along whether they're welcome or not, so I pick men who don't drive me to drink with their questions." He shrugged. "I reckon Mr. Short will do."

"Mr. Short is a capable writer."

Wyatt nodded in the direction Daisy had gone. "Looks like you lost a friend, if you don't mind my saying."

This was a strange man, talking with me like I was his equal. "I shouldn't have yelled at her; it wasn't her I was mad at."

"We all make mistakes," he said, the coin flicking back and forth over his fingers.

"That doesn't make it right."

"No, and it never will. It's been my experience that you have to be honest in your apology or women won't ever let you forget it." He spoke as if he were plenty experienced. "Honest in my apology," wasn't that what Pa said?

I glanced at his revolvers. "Are those six shooters?"

"That's right."

"They loaded?"

"Five rounds."

"Why only five?"

"Every practiced gun-wielder knows that Colts have a hair-trigger adjustment. You have to respect your weapons." I must have looked confused because he added, "The hammer rests on the empty chamber, Logan."

I looked at him carefully. He couldn't be more than 25 years old. He looked smart in his long moustache that reached his chin on each side before curling back toward his cheeks. His face was tanned and his eyes were dark under long, straight eyebrows. Everything about this man looked sharp, even his large, pointed nose. He hadn't smiled once during our conversation. He was serious, like Pa.

I wondered if he had ever killed a man. Swallowing, I lifted Daisy's books. "Good to meet you, Wyatt."

He nodded and went back to rocking. He took everything in under those dark eyebrows.

I made my way back down Douglas, wondering where Daisy was. I decided to check the Arkansas River. Wyatt had said "an honest apology." He'd probably had plenty of people backed against the wall that would say just about anything.

Daisy sat beneath a large tree that offered a canopy of

rust-colored leaves. She drew her knees to her chest and stared out over the river. "Go away, Logan."

I shook my head. "Daisy, you have to understand."

She looked up at me, her eyes red and swollen from crying. "I think you explained everything perfectly." She looked back out over the river again, and I stepped in front of her, holding her books out. When she didn't take them, I knelt down. "Daisy, please don't cry. I shouldn't have said that, and I didn't mean it. I don't even think of you as a girl."

She gasped. "Is that supposed to make me feel better?"

"I mean, I think of you as more than just a girl. I searched for something to say. *You have to be honest in your apology.*

"Daisy, you're my only true friend. I guess I took my bad news out on you because you were there. I don't mind your questions—that was dumb of me to say. Your questions are what make you special. You're not like other girls…you're different."

Daisy looked down at her hands as if they were the most interesting things she had ever seen. She checked her fingernails and straightened her dress before looking up. "What bad news?"

"Forget it," I said, shaking my head. "It's work and doesn't have a thing to do with us." I held out my hand to help her up.

She stared at me for a moment before slipping her hand into mine. Relieved, I held steady as she pulled herself up.

Just then, my back foot slid down the embankment. I grabbed for Daisy with my free hand, missing and losing my footing entirely. We both tumbled down the riverbank. I tried to slow our fall before we hit the water, but it was no use. We both plunged

into the cold water, kicking and clawing at the bank. Luckily, the current was slow and there were tree roots to grab on to. Daisy looked so surprised, I laughed before I could help myself.

"I suppose you think this is funny!" she cried, her braids floating behind her. She looked like a drowned cat.

She cupped her hand and splashed water in my face. "That's for saying I need girlfriends. And this…"

But she didn't get it out. I grabbed her and dunked her under the water. She came up sputtering, her teeth chattering. "Why, you, you…"

I grabbed her again, but she screamed, "Mercy!" and laughed as we crawled out of the river.

That night Mama cut paper dolls with Lizzie, I worked on my rewrite, and Pa smoked his pipe and hummed while working figures on paper to see how much fence we needed for Pilgrim. Mama started humming along, pulling Lizzie onto her lap and untying her braids. Pa put his pipe down and sneezed.

"Bless you," Mama said.

Pa sneezed again, twice, then again.

Lizzie chimed in, "Bless you, bless you, bless you." She flicked up a different finger each time she said it.

Something must have tickled his nose because Pa got to sneezing so hard he had to stand up. His sneezes came one on top of the other, and soon he was stamping his foot every time he sneezed. He reminded me of Pilgrim. Pa blinked hard and reached up to wipe away the tears from his eyes.

Lizzie ran out of fingers to count with and started giggling. And then we all got tickled. Mama's voice was full of laughter. "Bless us all!"

Pa threw his head back and laughed. We all went to bed grinning.

CHAPTER 12
A FAMILY PICTURE

That weekend Wichita held a fall festival. We woke early so we wouldn't miss what turned out to be the shortest parade I'd ever seen. But the city officials set up rides, races, and contests of every sort. Everybody seemed to want to try his or her luck at one contest or another. Mama baked a pumpkin pie for the pie contest.

People filled the streets. A man gave balloons to any child who wanted one. Occasionally one would slip away, its ribboned tail waving goodbye to the crying child left behind.

Whiffs of popcorn and roasted ears of corn filled the air, and Lizzie pulled at Pa's shirtsleeve until he thrust a small bag into her pudgy little hands. Mama tied Lizzie's balloon to her wrist, and every now and then, it would bop me square in the face.

A gunshot cracked through the music and chattering,

announcing the start of the sack race. Boys kicked a pig bladder back and forth in the street, weaving through the crowd. The sun rose to its mid-morning duty and warmed the chilly air.

Mama wandered over to the raffle drawing for donated quilts, a popcorn-fisted Lizzie bumping along behind her. Pa went to inspect the new farming machinery that lined the front of the mercantile. Groups of men in overalls ran their hands over the shiny plows.

The cowboys and herders seemed to be thoroughly enjoying themselves. They gambled on one another to see who would win the three-legged race. They were a noisy lot, clapping winners on the back, shoving losers into a nearby horse tank.

A photographer sat on a corner beside a makeshift tent, and cowboys peered at themselves in a looking glass before standing tall and sober to have their pictures made. I admired their bullhide chaps and boots with stirrups. A Mexican cowboy wore light-colored woolly chaps. I made a mental note to write Gramps and Gram about all this.

"Looks like a good time," Pa said, eyeing the cowboys as they posed in groups. "Why don't you fetch your mama and Lizzie, and we'll have the man take our photo?"

My eyebrows shot up. I ran quickly to fetch Mama.

The photographer arranged us outside of the tent. He offered Mama a stool, and Lizzie sat on her lap while Pa and I stood behind them. The photographer disappeared beneath the black curtain that hung from the back of his camera. We all stared directly into the open eyeball of the camera, which seemed to be peering deeply into our little family, taking us all in, ready to capture more than our images. The moment he told us to hold ten seconds, Pa laid his hand on my shoulder. I smiled before I could help it.

"Our first picture in Wichita," Pa said, helping Mama up. "Remember our last family picture?"

I thought for a moment. Our last picture was in St. Louis. I was nine, and Lizzie was a baby. Gramps and Gram were in the picture, but I didn't remember much else. "What about it?"

Mama explained. "The photographer arranged us for the portrait. Gram and I sat on stools with your pa and grandpa standing behind us. Lizzie was in my lap, and the photographer wanted you to stand between Gram and me. You waited until he turned around and ran over in front of your pa. You did that three times before the man finally gave up and let you stand on a stool by your pa."

Lizzie grinned. "You wouldn't sit still."

"I forgot that," I murmured. I glanced at Pa. He looked like he was replaying that day in his mind; maybe those memories brought comfort to the divide we felt today.

Pa paid for the photo, and I led Lizzie toward the hitching post, where I saw Daisy watching people scuttle down the street. Mama took Lizzie's hand and gave me permission to stay with Daisy. I made my way to where she was staring at a small family. I noticed the little girl was about Lizzie's age.

"Hello, Daisy."

She smiled thoughtfully. "Did you ever wonder what it would be like to be a plainsman?"

Always a question. I suppressed a smile and lifted a shoulder.

A look of disappointment passed fleetingly over her face. "Well, don't you have an idea?"

"Plowing, planting, gathering buffalo chips...sounds hard to beat."

She looked back at the family. The little girl had a dress fashioned from a feed sack. The mother wore a clean but well-worn calico dress, and both the boy and his pa were in wool pants.

Someone was playing "Camptown Races" on the piano. Chinese women pushed a cart of clean, pressed clothes. Two fashionable women chatted beneath their parasols, dressed in neck-high lace, gloves, and cameo pins. Their hair curled underneath their fancy hats. I thought about Mama's simple apparel. She had a nice silk dress and a heavy dress for winter.

"They don't look like they have enough to eat," Daisy commented, her eyes sad.

"It's amazing the difference between families, isn't it?" I agreed. "That's true everywhere, Daisy, even in St. Louis. Those people chose to be farmers. Some say those farmers using that new barbed wire to keep cattle and raise them here are going to put the range riders right out of business. Maybe we should feel sorry for the range riders instead."

Daisy shook her head, her brown braids swinging from side to side. "I could never give this up—the city is so exciting!"

"This is no city! The tallest building is the Occidental Hotel —three whole stories. They stick bison hair in the clay between the wood planks to strengthen the walls," I scoffed. "St. Louis— now there's a city."

"Sod is the new Kansas marble, or did you know that, too, Mister Reporter?"

I ignored that, telling her instead about all the things I missed in St. Louis: art collections, horse races, theater, and most of all, Gram and Gramps. "But Pa had to bring us here, had to take us away from all of that," I sighed.

"Funny, your pa told me he wanted to add to your experiences by bringing you to Wichita," Daisy murmured, looking down at her shoes.

"When did he say that?"

"Yesterday," she replied. "Don't look so surprised. I like to spend time with your parents after school."

I shrugged. Why should I be surprised? I wasn't jealous.

Was I?

CHAPTER 13

PRIORITIES

It was late October and you could almost taste the cold in your mouth. Even with the bright autumn sun, a permanent chill had settled on the pumpkin, and I kept my collar up against the cold on my way home from work.

Passing our garden, I noticed someone had picked the weeds and tended the vegetables. Pa waited up ahead by the woodpile, another chore I had failed to complete.

"Sorry, Pa," I called, walking quickly. "I know I'm late again, but we were working on a story..."

"I will not hear anymore." His voice was low. "Logan, your mama and I work hard to keep this house functioning. Our home is a priority." He coughed hard into his hand. Clearing his throat, he looked at me. "Do I make myself clear?"

"Yes, sir."

"You will tell Mr. Murdock you can only work after your chores are finished," Pa stated flatly.

My neck burned and my cheeks colored. "I can't do that, Pa."

"You can't?" His voice sounded strangled.

"I…I won't."

He looked like he might explode. But he started coughing instead, and he took a few steps toward me. His arm was out and he grabbed my shoulder. I thought sure I was in for a whipping until I saw his face. He was pale, ghostly white. He leaned on me for a moment and then collapsed to the ground.

"Pa! Mama, come quick!"

The front door swung wide and Mama squinted, trying to adjust to the dark. "Cyrus!" In one swift movement, she fell to her knees beside him, cupping his face in her hands. "Logan, fetch some water from the barrel," she ordered.

I ran to the back of the house and grabbed the bucket, spooning water for Pa. When I returned, he was sitting up against the woodpile as Mama wiped his forehead with her apron. I handed him the water. He took a few sips and nodded faintly when Mama insisted on having Dr. Kramer come by.

"I will go to him," Pa said, too proud even now to trouble another.

Mama hesitated, searching his face. She nodded reluctantly and helped him to his feet. "Stay with Lizzie," she said to me.

I watched as they slowly made their way down the road, Pa stopping occasionally to rest but determined to continue. I heard his coughing from the front porch. When I lost their shapes in the darkness, I went inside.

Lizzie was in her room, playing with her paper dolls. She looked up at me. "Oh, it's only you."

"Lizzie, Mama and Pa went for a walk. I'm in charge now, and it's time for bed."

"NO!" she cried, her little mouth making an O.

"Come on. I'll tell you a story."

She debated this. Finally she told her dolls good night, and I tucked her into bed. She was fast asleep before I was halfway through an Indian princess story.

I returned to the family room, determined to wait up for my parents. I thought about what Pa said before his spell. He had been taking up my slack. I sat in Pa's chair, his empty pipe nearby.

The *Eagle* printed my rewrite about Joshua Gunn, and Mama framed it. Now it was beside Pa's pipe. There was something else— a piece of paper. At first, I thought it was Lizzie's handwriting, but it wasn't. Someone had written above a line and then left room for another to copy. I read:

The boy can run and play. I see a boy and a girl.

My mouth went dry. Daisy said she had been here. I recognized her writing on the top line, but who copied the phrase so painstakingly below the line? Could it be?

Then I noticed my old *McGuffey's Reader*. I sat in Pa's chair with the book on my lap, trying to imagine what it felt like for him to learn how to read. I pictured him concentrating on sounding out words, the crease above his nose deepening. How could a man with so much pride allow Daisy to teach him? Who else knew? Surely Mama, maybe Lizzie, but not me. Not me.

CHAPTER 14

LEAVING A MARK

Dr. Kramer prescribed an elixir for Pa and told him to rest for a good long week. Pa took the medicine and went back to work the next day. I decided not to mention the *McGuffey's Reader* and made sure I finished my chores.

"Logan, I have a story that needs attention," Mr. Murdock announced as soon as I got to work. "Come in and close the door, son," he instructed, settling behind his desk and smoking his cigar. He began scribbling furiously.

It was difficult to wait, so I busied myself with looking at all the awards on his desk for high merit and excellence in journalism. I glanced at Mr. Murdock, still engrossed in his writing. I tried to imagine myself sitting behind that desk one day. Mr. Murdock looked disheveled, his white shirt half-tucked and falling out below the plaid vest, his sleeves banded around his forearms. His trousers sported the stains of his own inky fingerprints. The thin glasses at the end of his nose slipped every time he bent down, and his tousled hair looked like something a mother would slick down as soon as he rolled out of bed. Obviously Mr. Murdock's mother didn't live with him anymore.

He finally stopped writing and smiled. "Yes," he said, nodding and holding the paper up to the window. He shot a look at me and picked up a new cigar, biting the end off. He leaned back and lifted his feet onto the desk.

"Nothing like a good ending, eh, Logan?"

"Sir?"

"I wonder if you might know the Nichols boy, Ethan? You probably go to school with some of that tribe."

I leaned forward. "Yes, sir. I know Ethan. Why?"

"Seems young Mr. Nichols was out late a few nights back. The sheriff ran into him behind Connie's Kitchen and felt determined to return him safely home, when the boy struggled and became resistant. Said he didn't need ushering and could manage to get home on his own. Well, we all know our fine officer of the law wouldn't take some scrap boy's word on things. No, he needed to make sure the boy's parents knew their son was out so late."

Mr. Murdock's chair groaned as he stretched back in it. "Now Sheriff Lahey discovered that no one was home at the Nichols's. In fact, he found the entire family, Mr. and Mrs. Nichols and Ethan and his three younger sisters, living in their wagon behind the hotel. Mr. Nichols has reportedly been out of work for three weeks. They have no family here in Kansas to lean on." He hesitated and narrowed his eyes at me, "You weren't aware of this, were you?"

I shook my head.

"Well, the church will be sending around the offering plate for the homeless family next Sunday. Seems the sheriff had a glisten in his eye when he saw the youngest, Jessie, only three, with mussed hair and dirty clothes, hungrier than a stray cat. This article needs to run in this week's paper. I have to admit I feel pride knowing this paper will help return that family to good standing. It sends a message to Mr. Earp, our new assistant deputy, that we take care of our own here in Wichita."

He laid his cigar in a silver tray. "Have it on my desk by Wednesday. Our readers will be happy to help a neighbor in need. I bet that within a week, Mr. Nichols will have a job and the family will have a place to sleep." He sighed happily. "That's what good reporting does for the soul."

"Yes, sir." I couldn't get the frown off my face. Ethan would probably rather hang by his thumbs than see his family's story all over the town paper. He might be poor and not particularly fascinating, but one thing I knew for sure: Ethan Nichols was proud.

"Here's some of what I've gathered already, although I don't think it'll do you much good. That Nichols boy just bragged about some potato race he won. You'll have to follow up," he said. "I want the story to be written from a youngster's perspective. Give me emo-emo-emo!"

"Excuse me?"

Mr. Murdock raised an eyebrow. "How long have you been here, boy?"

I knew when he called me "boy," he wasn't happy.

"Six weeks."

"I want EMOTION-EMOTION-EMOTION!" bellowed Mr. Murdock, his face determined as his fist came down, upsetting his cigar all over his desk. "Blast!" he growled and grabbed his notes. Brushing them off, he handed them to me. "Don't give me less than your best, boy."

He motioned me out of his office, and I reluctantly took the papers over to Mr. Short's desk, since he was out of the office. I began reading over the notes. How could I keep my job and not humiliate my friend? I wished I had someone to ask. I desperately needed Gramps.

I swept the office and galley-proofed a few advertisements before grabbing my pack. I needed to clear my head, and riding Pilgrim seemed just the thing. On my way to the stables, I passed Pa's blacksmith shop and decided to stop and tell him.

Mr. Armstrong, his boss, was hammering away at a horseshoe.

"Mr. Armstrong, have you seen my pa?" I asked, scanning the small room.

The older man grabbed the horseshoe with a pair of tongs, heading back for the fire pit. His work area was a waist-high table with red-hot coals piled to one side, near the opening of a small brick chimney. Tools of all sorts hung on pegs or filled toolboxes. A comforting warmth filled the smoky, dark room. I understood why Pa liked working here.

"Your pa left early. He can't seem to shake that cough," Mr. Armstrong said, stirring the coals.

"He went home?" I could not recall a time Pa had ever missed a day of work.

"I told him to stay home until he was completely cured," the blacksmith explained. His hands were covered in soot, and I suspected that, like Pa's, they also bore the scars of getting too close to the fire.

I decided that if Pa was sick enough to be home, I should probably be there as well. I headed home, my hands deep in my pockets and my head down. My thoughts turned from Pa to Ethan.

Pa rested in bed and I watched Lizzie while Mama worked in the kitchen. Lizzie grew bored with me and squealed with delight at the sight of Daisy at the front door. She held up her doll. "Wanna play?" she asked.

"I need to talk to your brother, okay?" Daisy answered.

Lizzie shrugged but didn't budge.

"Lizzie," I said, opening the door for Daisy, "Two's company, three's a crowd."

She crossed her arms over her chest and answered, "And four and five are nine!"

I gave her a stern look and walked outside with Daisy. "What's up?"

Daisy handed me a rock. It was almost white, big enough to fill my palm, and when I rolled it over, I saw why it was important. It was a fossil. There was a perfect imprint of a small fish.

"I found it by the river. Daddy took me there yesterday to fish. He invited Ethan Nichols and his sisters. Daddy said to tell your pa to stop by for some fish—what with there being so much and all, he aims to share. Truth be told, Daddy doesn't even care for fish—he just likes the quiet time," Daisy rambled.

"What are you going to do with this?" I asked, handing the fossil back.

Daisy hesitated. "I thought your pa might like it."

"Pa?"

She shifted her feet. "Why not?" she asked in a hushed voice.

"Why Pa?"

"Why NOT?" she asked again, her voice angry. "You know, Logan, your pa works as hard as anyone I know. He might not be your hero, but you don't give him a chance…" She stopped short, her face red.

"Daisy?"

"Forget it," she said, handing the fossil back. "Please give this to him when he gets home."

"He's home now. He can't shake his cough."

She looked at me for a long moment, her face sad. "Good night, Logan."

That night, I focused my attention on the article. I still had not figured out how to save Ethan's pride and my job. I sat at the kitchen table, staring at the blank page.

"Trouble?" Pa asked, over my shoulder. I didn't figure he'd know what to do, but then I remembered Daisy's words—*you don't give him a chance.*

I told him my problem. As usual, Pa only listened, nodding occasionally but saying nothing. I expected him to wish me luck and leave the room.

Instead, Pa sat down. "Do you want to keep your job, even if it means doing something you're not comfortable with?"

I thought for a minute. It was true. Journalism didn't always seem like a respectable profession when people reported private things. "I think it depends, Pa."

"Meaning what?"

"Like with my first story. If you start out by muddin' up the waters, you'll think that's okay, and the next time, the fibbing might come easier, and soon you'll be writing fiction. But if you start out writing the truth, you'll be more respected, even if it's only by yourself."

"That might get lonely."

"What I don't understand is that there are plenty of stories out there, so why make news out of another's misfortune?" We were both quiet for a moment. Then I added, "I suppose if we all looked at it that way, the *Eagle* would only print happy endings. Pa, I can't write this article like Ethan and his family are destitute, but I can't protect him just because he might get embarrassed either. It's a story, and I have to tell it."

"Didn't you say Mr. Murdock wanted this from a child's perspective?" Pa asked, chewing thoughtfully on a toothpick.

"Yes, sir."

"Well, it might be high adventure living on the street—I mean from a child's way of seeing things," Pa went on.

It was like the flash of lightning from the night we lost Pilgrim. "That's it! Thanks, Pa!" I said, grabbing my pencil and paper.

Pa scooted his chair back. He coughed before saying, "I'll leave you to it, then."

I hardly noticed him leave—I was so bent on trying out this

new angle. Using the notes Mr. Murdock gave me, I wrote:

Ethan Nichols is a well-liked student with an eye for adventure and an amazing talent for turning his luck around. After what seemed like a bad turn, what with his pa being injured at our mill and Mr. Lewis firing him instead of allowing him to take the proper time to heal, the Nichols family pulled together. "God will provide," Mrs. Nichols assured. "We have our wagon and team. We have each other," Mr. Nichols reminded.

That's when Ethan decided to enter last Saturday's potato race. Ethan picked up and deposited all ten potatoes in a basket and had it sitting on the judge's stand almost before his opponents crossed the starting line. It's amazing the speed one can have when given the right motivation. Ethan easily won the race and the $5.00 in gold, while his father won an equal sum in a wager on his son. Father and son, working together, brought home $10 to add to the family fund.

Sheriff Lahey stumbled across Ethan later that evening and escorted him home, discovering the family situation. He is calling on all the fine citizens of Wichita to add what they can to the offering plate on Sunday to help the family.

This reporter isn't too sure the Nichols family will accept such generosity, as they have a way of landing on their feet. Just yesterday Ethan devised a pulley for his friends who were building a tree house and needed a way to lift the lumber. Necessity is the mother of invention. Who knows, Ethan Nichols may be the next Samuel Morse.

I would have to check some facts, but I was writing. I stood up to stretch and heard a soft thud. It was Daisy's fossil, which I had forgotten to give to Pa. I grabbed it and walked into the other room. Pa was asleep in his chair, my old *McGuffey's Reader* open in his lap. The clinking of Mama's knitting needles caught my attention, and we looked at each other for a moment. She winked at me and smiled.

"What do you have there?" she whispered.

"Daisy wanted me to give Pa this fossil she found at the river yesterday, but I forgot."

I handed it to Mama. She smiled. "Something left its mark behind, didn't it?" She had a wistful look when she gave it back to me. "It will keep until tomorrow. Let him sleep. He needs his rest."

I could count on one hand the number of times I'd seen Pa asleep before the rest of us.

"Good night, Mama," I whispered, kissing her cheek.

She touched my hand. "You're growing up fast, young man. I'm proud of you." She glanced at Pa. "We both are."

My back stiffened. "You don't have to speak for him."

Mama put her knitting down. "He doesn't always know how to say it, honey."

I looked at Pa, studying his face for a moment. It was usually so stern, but now it seemed slack and soft. As I passed his chair, I tucked the fossil in his hands before climbing the stairs to bed.

CHAPTER 15
ROLE MODELS

"Look at the big reporter," Daisy teased, landing a light punch on my arm.

I rolled my eyes and grabbed the paper from her. We were at Connie's Kitchen, sipping sarsaparilla and celebrating the printing of my story. Ethan liked my version of his family's tribulations, and Mr. Murdock, although not terribly pleased, accepted it on the condition that I do a follow-up on the success of the community's generosity.

"The real success story came last night." I told Daisy how Mama asked me to read my article to the family. "I picked up the paper and was about to start reading when Pa interrupted. 'Why don't I give it a go?' he asked, and I think I grinned so big I embarrassed him."

I looked around at the other customers before going on. "He

did it, Daisy. He read every word. He stumbled and was sort of slow, but..." I grabbed her hand and smiled. "You made this possible. Thanks, Daisy."

Daisy's cheeks turned bright pink, and she looked down at our hands on the table. She squeezed mine before sliding hers back to her lap. "Your pa did all the work. You know, I don't think he really thought he could, as if he was sure he was a tad shy of intelligence. There are probably scads of people out there who don't realize their own potential. The fear of failure is powerfully strong. I hope to change that one day."

I grinned. Daisy would change the world.

Pa's health worsened. It seemed like one day he was out banging nails and the next day he was shivering so hard that he couldn't sit still. Mama made his favorite stew and cornbread, but when he didn't eat it, lines of worry creased her forehead. He tried to rest in his chair but gave up and went to bed, where he tossed and turned under the warm quilt. Mama sent me to fetch Dr. Kramer, even though Pa grumbled about the late hour.

I stayed in the parlor by the fire with Mama while Dr. Kramer examined Pa. Although I ate more than my share of stew, my stomach felt empty. I wanted to say something to comfort Mama, but I couldn't think of a single thing. Lizzie played quietly with her dominoes, understanding that Pa was sick. When Dr. Kramer finally emerged, his face was solemn. Mama waited for him to speak.

"Mable, I'm afraid it's pneumonia. Cyrus said he was out in that storm a while back." He shook his head. "I wish he would have rested when I told him to."

Mama's voice faltered when she asked if Pa would recover.

Dr. Kramer's silence said everything. He glanced at her before studying the fire. I followed his gaze and stood mesmerized by the flames licking the log. He was out in that storm a while back. I thought of Pa sending me in to my warm bed while he searched for Pilgrim, then his sneezing and how we all thought it was so funny. He had collapsed while scolding me for not helping with chores.

It was a long time before Dr. Kramer finally spoke.

"We'll see."

Mama decided I shouldn't work at the *Eagle* until Pa recovered. She needed me at home and that was that. I was to tell Mr. Murdock after school and come straight home.

I knew it wasn't right, but I felt angry. Angry at myself for not tying Pilgrim properly that day, angry at Pa for not resting when Dr. Kramer told him to, angry at Mama for not realizing how important my job was, and most of all, angry about having to be here in Wichita in the first place. If we still lived in St. Louis, none of this would have happened.

Daisy caught me after school. "Logan, wait. I'll walk with you," she said quietly. We walked in silence to the *Eagle*. I didn't feel like talking and was amazed at how well Daisy knew my moods. I rolled around different versions of how I'd tell Mr. Murdock goodbye without having feelings in front of him.

"I'll wait out here," Daisy offered when we got to the shop.

The shop was abuzz with news. Mr. Short and Mr. Whitney were deep in conversation and didn't even look up when I entered.

The slapping of the press and the smell of ink seemed to lull me away from reality. I wanted to close the shop door behind me and forget what I was here to do. Maybe Mr. Murdock had a good lead on a story he wanted me to write.

I shook my head. Mama needed me at home. I sighed and knocked on Mr. Murdock's office door. He looked up quickly, setting his pen down, noticing my concern. "Logan, what is it?"

This was it. I had to tell him I was to go home and be the man of the house. My priorities had changed.

Mr. Murdock rose from his chair and came around the desk. "What's the matter, son? What's happened?"

His voice was full of concern. I'd never seen him like this before, and it was all I could take. Tears slid down my cheeks before I could help it. I stood there staring at him, betrayed by my own tears.

Mr. Murdock closed the door behind me. He drew the shade and gestured for me to sit.

Finally, I found my voice. "Pa has pneumonia. Mama needs me at home."

Leaning against his desk, he nodded slowly, processing this information. He cleared his throat before he spoke. "Logan, it's important to remember one thing as a journalist. The paper always comes first."

My eyes widened. I think he saw my startled look because he rushed on. "That is, the paper always comes first unless your family has to. This is a case where it is obvious that you must temporarily put your family first. You are quite right to be there for your mother. Your immediate goals must be set aside until this matter is cleared up. Then, and only then, will you be of any use to the *Wichita City Eagle*."

I blinked. Was he trying to make me feel worse? I brushed my tears from my cheeks with my shirtsleeve and stood up. "This matter that needs clearing up could end in Pa's death," I said evenly. "Then I don't care what you print in your newspaper, Mr. Murdock. He'll never be able to read it again."

He called after me as I stormed out of his office. Outside, I found Daisy watching people come and go from the saloon across the street. I wiped my eyes before she turned around. "Daisy, I need to get home. Sorry, I can't talk."

I turned towards home. I decided to make one more stop. I found myself at the stables and went to Pilgrim's stall.

"I may not be able to ride you for a while, boy," I said, petting his nose. He heaved a big sigh as if he understood. "Pa's real sick...he might not..." I couldn't finish. Pilgrim stood still. "I'll come by and see you every day, okay?"

Being near Pilgrim made me feel better. Pa had picked him out for me, and even though I didn't like the way he'd paid for him, I couldn't ignore the fact that he'd tried to do something nice. Why had I been so angry? Why couldn't I accept his way of doing things? I couldn't answer those questions.

Mama worked round the clock, sleeping only when Pa rested. A pot of water remained on the stove where she boiled hot rags and then cooled them slightly before wringing them out with her bare hands and laying them over Pa's chest.

Dr. Kramer came every day. He left a bromide mixture for Pa

and assured Mama they were doing everything possible. Pa coughed terribly, and Dr. Kramer propped him up on pillows so he could breathe easier.

I stood in the doorway on Friday afternoon and watched Pa sleep. He tossed the covers off and rubbed his bleary eyes. "Son," he whispered.

"Hi, Pa. Are you feeling any better?"

He started to speak but gagged and coughed into his fist, shaking his head. After the fit, he sank back into his pillows. "The fence," he began, but had to stop and swallow away the urge to cough again.

"I know, Pa. It's Friday. I'm going to spend tomorrow working on it. You have all the supplies ready. Don't worry."

His face was pale and his eyes looked dark with trouble. He stared at me for a moment before nodding. Then his eyes slid closed and he turned away.

CHAPTER 16

PA'S DECISION

After waking up early the next morning, I headed for the barn, picked up Pa's hammer, and began to pound away at my fear. I was so caught up in hammering the boards to the fence posts, trying to keep them level and even, I soon forgot about Mr. Murdock and the *Eagle*, about Wichita, and even about Pa a little bit. No wonder he enjoyed this work so much—you could get lost in it. I wondered if he ever tried to forget about things when he hammered. My back was sore from bending so much, and I welcomed the break when Mama called me in for a sandwich.

"Your pa will be so happy when he gets well and sees that fence. It's a comfort to him to know you are helping out at home, Logan," she said, smiling her most confident smile. I knew she didn't honestly feel that cheerful.

Lizzie had been acting strange ever since Pa fell ill. She cried if any of us raised our voice to her, but Mama told me it was normal, what with her being only six and all.

The afternoon raced by, and when I stood back and looked at how much I had accomplished, I smiled. Granted, all the fence posts had already been set, so it was only a matter of nailing the boards up between them, but it was a good start. I reported all this to Pa, watching as he sipped broth from Mama's spoon. He nodded weakly.

"Get better soon, Pa," I said in a feeble voice. I read to Lizzie from David Copperfield and heated up water for baths. Mama bathed Lizzie in the kitchen bath and then took her to bed. Then it was my turn, and I soaked in the tub until the water went cold. My body felt as if I had worked all week on the fence, instead of just one day. I emptied the tub and tipped it on its side against the back porch to dry. I fell asleep almost as soon as my head hit the pillow.

Sunday morning, Mama announced that we would not be attending church service, but it was a good idea to say a prayer for Pa. Dr. Kramer came by before church, and Reverend Randall stopped by afterward. Once word got out about Pa's illness, our neighbors stopped in one after another to leave baked goods, preserves, and fully cooked meals. Mrs. Cox came to fetch Lizzie for the day to play with her little girl, Lily. Lizzie seemed a bit shy until Lily mentioned a dollhouse her pa had built. Then she merely kissed Mama's cheek and waved goodbye.

Reverend Randall had suggested to his congregation that I might need help with the fence, and that afternoon, three of my classmates were hammering away beside me. Ethan Nichols was among them. The tables had turned, it seemed, and I wondered if the paper would report Pa's illness.

We finished by midday, and I sat on the porch, enjoying lemonade. I offered it around. When we heard Pa's rattling cough, our visitors fell silent. Mama ran in to help Pa, and our guests quickly and quietly made their exit. I sat alone, listening to the cough wrack Pa's body until I thought he would pass out from pure exhaustion.

Locusts buzzed in the afternoon sun. The sky stretched wide across the open expanse of the Kansas prairie. This might be a growing town, but it had only been a few years since buffalo grazed here. I was suddenly aware of the changes this land was undergoing and felt strange to be a part of it.

The wind picked up, rustling over the ground and rolling tumbleweeds as it blew. Mama's red and yellow chrysanthemums swayed back and forth as if dodging the bees that tried to land on them. The town itself seemed abnormally quiet. *Sunday afternoon, people must be inside with their families.* Now that Pa was quiet, I heard Mama in the kitchen. I closed my eyes and listened to Kansas and its earthy nature music.

Then I heard a buckboard coming down the road and opened my eyes to see Mr. Murdock stop in front of our house and hop down. He grabbed his hat off his head and held it in both hands. "Logan, how is your father?"

"No better, sir."

He sighed and seemed to be struggling with what to say next.

Finally he shook his head and went on. "I came because I have something to ask you."

Mama came to the door and greeted Mr. Murdock quietly, asking if he would care to come in for a cup of fresh coffee.

"Thank you, ma'am. That would be fine," he said.

In the parlor, she served Mr. Murdock coffee along with sugar cookies that one of the neighbors had brought. "Mrs. Peterson made these. Please take two."

Mr. Murdock must have realized he'd come empty-handed because he paused, but then thanked Mama and took the cookies.

"I hoped Mr. West would be back on his feet by now, ma'am. I'm afraid my visit is a waste of time, and time is of the essence in this situation."

"What situation?"

"The Tisdale stage was robbed an hour ago," Mr. Murdock reported. "The scoundrels waited until Sunday afternoon when most people are at home. Only the driver can identify them, and he is having a tough time seeing out of two swollen eyes at present. Mr. Moser and his partners are stating their loss at more than two hundred dollars. He asked that Mr. Earp and Mr. Behrens, our fine deputies, ride after the men and bring them back to Wichita."

Mama interrupted him. "I'm afraid I don't understand what that has to do with us, Mr. Murdock. Logan already told you he can't work."

"Mrs. West, I'm too old to be following men on horseback into Oklahoma Territory myself, and unfortunately, Mr. Short is on his way to Dodge City to follow up on another story entirely. I hoped

Logan could get this story. I spoke with Mr. Earp, told him I wanted to send a reporter. He's not champing at the bit to take such a greenhorn, but he finally agreed—though he did demand final editing privileges before we ran the story. It seems he might make a small sum by selling the story elsewhere." Mr. Murdock laughed nervously.

I held my breath, praying she would let me go.

Mama looked flabbergasted. "Mr. Murdock, I think you made a mistake. Logan has no experience riding across the countryside in search of outlaws. I don't even know how to prepare a child for something like that."

"Mable."

We were all startled to see Pa in the doorway. He looked like he might collapse. Mr. Murdock jumped up and helped him to a chair.

Mama ran to fetch his blanket to put across his legs. Pa leaned back in his chair and took a moment to gather his strength before speaking. "Will my son be in danger?"

"Sir, no more danger than any other man, and I feel confident in saying that Mr. Earp and Mr. Behrens are afraid of nothing and nobody," Mr. Murdock insisted. "The journey would be no trouble. They plan to ride all night, hoping to catch up with the thieves before they reach Indian Territory." He caught Mama's reaction to this and added quickly, "Word has been sent to all the telegraph stations along the road, and Mr. Earp assures me he will not follow them past the Oklahoma line."

"Cyrus," Mama started, but Pa put up his hand to silence her, and she bit back whatever else she was about to say.

Pa turned to me. His eyes were red-rimmed but sharp. "Do you want to go, son?"

I went to him and knelt beside his chair. I didn't care if Mr. Murdock saw. I looked up at Pa. "Maybe I shouldn't leave you right now, Pa."

"I didn't ask that. I asked if you wanted to go."

I knew what he was asking, but I didn't know how to answer him until I remembered what he said about being honest. "Yes, sir," I answered.

Pa turned to Mama. "Let him go," he said simply. Mama gasped, and Mr. Murdock flicked his hat against his knee in success.

I hugged Pa. Mr. Murdock jumped up and said, "Time's a-wasting, Logan. You'll need to pack provisions and saddle your horse. Meet back at city hall as soon as you're ready." He nodded and tipped his hat at Mama on his way out the door. He turned around and added, "Be sure to bring your rifle."

CHAPTER 17
THE LONG RIDE

The next ten minutes were a blur. I helped Pa back to bed, and he leaned against his pillows, exhausted. Mama didn't say a word, but her clattering in the kitchen got louder as she packed food for me while I tended my rifle. I rolled my blanket tight before tying it with a leather strap and remembered the trading beads at the last minute. I heard Mama speaking with Pa, and then she appeared by my side, resting my bag on the floor.

"Logan, please be careful," she whispered, holding me so tightly I had to loosen her grip. She laughed nervously and held my shoulders. "I don't know why I'm so afraid," she said. "You're almost grown. You have a good head on your shoulders." She hugged me again. "Be careful."

"I will, Mama."

I hugged them both goodbye, carried my bag and rifle to the

stable to fetch Pilgrim, and then went to city hall. I admit I felt tall in my saddle.

Wyatt nodded hello to me as I rode up. He mounted his own horse, an Appaloosa. He introduced Mr. John Behrens, already astride his dark mare, and we reached over and shook hands. It was only the three of us. My stomach churned. Pilgrim seemed to sense my discomfort. He stood perfectly still, waiting for my command.

"Let's ride," Wyatt said. We put spurs to our horses, leaving the safety of Wichita behind.

Before long I realized how deserted the prairie could be. We rode for miles, and the only other sign of human life was the wagon trails that stretched out as far as the eye could see.

The landscape could be painted in a few strokes of an artist's brush. I made mental notes so that I could tell Pa. The clay red soil hadn't budged beneath herds of bison, let alone the hooves of a few horses. Then there was the more complicated mixing of autumn reds, yellows, and browns of the turning grasses. The late-afternoon sky matched Mama's Wedgewood plates, beckoning you to widen your eyes and follow it across the open prairie.

Sometimes when I looked out at the prairie, I was mesmerized by the tall bluestem grass stretching up to the sky as the wind rushed across, creating waves. It reminded me of how Mama described the ocean, and I imagined this as the ocean of Kansas. The sun left bright patches of light where clouds weren't filtering above. Red-tailed hawks flew over the waves of grass, hunting food and diving when they spied it. I spotted a prairie dog village, with the little varmints poking their heads up far enough to watch us pass by. A pair of them seemed to be kissing or sniffing each other before pushing off with their front paws and chittering madly, bushing up their tails. Pilgrim, following Wyatt's Appaloosa, ignored them completely,

The air blew all around us, ruffling my hair. It was easy to picture flying a kite and running through the grass, trampling it down. The blue sky was the widest I'd ever seen and wrapped itself around us with its openness. I shuddered to think what it would be like if that sky ever turned on us. Kansas may not provide an ocean or mountains, but it had plenty of beauty all its own.

Wyatt slowed his horse to a walk, and I saw a gravesite alongside a wagon trail we had been following. A small pile of stones marked a grave of someone less fortunate who had tried to conquer this trail, someone who wanted to "see the elephant." Maybe someone like me.

Wyatt and Mr. Behrens didn't seem to care if I kept up with them or not. I nudged Pilgrim on and kept close as the sun slid past the horizon for the night. I assumed the cattle trail would lead us all the way to Oklahoma Territory, but Wyatt must have felt the bandits wouldn't keep to that trail because we rode well west of it. A huge harvest moon rose in the east, and I kept looking over my shoulder at it. We stopped at a river's edge to let the horses drink and because Mr. Behrens found a campfire that had been doused.

"Looks like we're on the right track," he said, pulling a stick from the ashes and touching the end gingerly.

Wyatt looked at me. "You holding up?"

"Yes, thank you. Thank you too, Mr. Behrens."

Wyatt snorted. "Just call him John, although he's partial to Johnny B." He smiled faintly but then grew serious. He nudged the ashes with his foot and rolled up a few red embers. "What say, John? Must be two, maybe three hours ahead?"

"They had that when we left Wichita. It took some time to make camp here." He threw the stick down. "We might catch up if we push on."

Wyatt nodded and fingered his pistol. "We'll use first light to jump." He went to fetch his horse.

John turned to me. It was hard to see his face in the shade of night, but I could see he was studying me. "You hang back when we meet up with these men. You're here to get your story, but in no way are you to be interferin', understand?"

I nodded. "Yes, sir." My voice cracked, so I cleared my throat and tried again. "Yes, sir."

I wish I would have listened.

CHAPTER 18

TRAPS

We rode into the night. There were times Wyatt or John would abruptly hold up a hand, and I would pull Pilgrim up. I felt sure the trail had grown cold. We had seen neither hide nor hair of the thieves, and at one point, I felt sure they had circled around and were now following us. I pulled the collar of my coat higher against my neck.

Up ahead, John reined in his horse. Wyatt and I stopped. Pilgrim perked his ears and stamped the ground. "It's okay, boy," I whispered, patting his neck to keep him quiet.

Then I heard it—the unmistakable sound of singing.

Oh Susannah,
Oh, don't you cry for me.
I've come from Alabama
with a banjo on my knee.

Wyatt slid off his horse and handed me the reins. John did the same, and they crept off toward the campsite on foot. I wasn't sure if I should dismount too or be ready to ride. What were they going to do—jump the men?

My heart pounded so hard, I imagined it echoing through the tall grass. I decided that if I heard gunshots, I would ride all three horses in. Then I remembered John's words. *In no way are you to be interferin'.*

What story could I get, back here holding the horses? If it were Mr. Short, he'd be off his mount, backing Wyatt. I had to act like a reporter. If I was ever to be more than a printer's devil, I needed this story.

Dismounting, I tethered all three horses to a nearby tree. I pulled my rifle down. Every book I'd ever read about Indians and how stealthily they moved came back to me. I crept silently in the direction the deputies had taken.

Blood pounded in my ears. I tried to swallow, but my mouth was too dry. I crouched low in the grass, moving slowly forward.

The men singing were obviously drunk. They slurred the words of the song and got completely lost in the melody. Finally, I made out the orange and white flames of their fire. There were two young men on either side of it, sitting on rocks, and passing a brown bottle back and forth. A short shovel leaned against a rock behind one of the men.

I was about to move forward to get a better look when suddenly, a hand clamped over my mouth and someone dragged me off my feet. My rifle fell. I grabbed for it, but rough hands jerked my arms and twisted them behind my back. My nerves screamed, but I couldn't make a sound. Eyes bulging, I whirled around to meet my captor.

"Good grief!" Wyatt muttered. His breath came fast, as if he had been running. He pointed to the ground in front of us. A trap lay wide open, ready to clamp down on my next step. *They must have put out the traps before they set up camp.* My mind raced. How many more were there? I stared at the trap, open and ready to snap my ankle in two.

Wyatt took his hand from my mouth but kept my arms behind me as he grabbed my rifle and pushed me away from the men. I wasn't surprised to see John back with the horses, anger written on his face. Wyatt shoved me in the direction of my horse. He turned to John. "He was ten feet away from them. Ten feet."

John shook his head. "Greenhorn."

I didn't reply. Wyatt gathered his reins and stepped up into his saddle. I felt about as big as Lizzie looking up at him.

"You better learn to listen first and ask those questions of yours after," Wyatt grumbled. He looked in the direction of the bandits. "Those men have staked out the area and laid traps and low wires. No matter how drunk they are, they're going to be loaded for bear if they hear one of those traps go. A drunken cowboy is ten times more dangerous than a sober one."

John nodded at me. "We've done this once or twice before. Watch and learn or you'll be getting more of a story than you bargained for, hear?" He spat at the ground.

"Yes, sir," I said quietly.

"Enough said," Wyatt said. "We'll fall back another quarter

mile and wait. They'll be pullin' up stakes and gatherin' snares by first light. We won't wait too long, though. I want them hurtin'."

We didn't make a fire. I pulled down my bedroll and crawled inside, trying to keep warm. My saddlebag made for a pillow. Punching it into place, a small piece of paper dropped out. I picked it up and held it to the moonlight, trying to see the words. It was nearly impossible to read, but it was unmistakably my father's childlike handwriting.

Dear Logan,

Keep safe. I am proud of you.

Pa

I stared at the note. Here I was, in pursuit of a story, my horse and rifle by my side. This is what Pa wanted for me. He may never be able to experience this, but he made darn sure I would. If I could have sent a note back to my father, I would have used the same two sentences. I turned my back to Wyatt and John, tears sliding down my nose, realizing that Pa had given me the freedom to write my own story.

A deep chill from the ground seeped through my blanket. I shivered, my body trying its best to create more heat. Finally the first hint of light brushed the eastern sky.

We were ready to go within minutes, our bedrolls tied back on our saddles. My stomach growled. Wyatt took pity on me and handed me a pouch with jerky tucked inside. "Hang back here," Wyatt instructed, looking at the creeping sun. "They may have picked those traps up by now and be near ready to ride." He turned to John. "I reckon they won't stop until they reach the border."

John grunted. "Let's do this thing."

They both looked at me.

"I'll stay here," I promised.

They checked their pistols before mounting their horses and riding off.

I turned to Pilgrim and patted his neck. I reached into my saddlebag for my writing supplies. Sitting on the ground, I took out my knife and sharpened the pencil. Then I wrote a few notes.

Wyatt Earp travels with a purpose. Mr. Earp and Mr. Behrens spoke very little as we crossed the vast expanse of prairie, searching for the Tisdale stage bandits. We knew only that they were armed and dangerous men. Not too shy on intelligence either as this reporter found out. The thieves set steel traps around their makeshift campsite.

I chewed on the stub of my pencil and added:

Notes: We saw prairie dogs, red-tailed hawks, blue jays, bull snakes, deer, coyotes, one bobcat.

This probably wouldn't go in my final story, but I wanted to remember these details in my journal.

I scribbled away, trying to get it all down when a high-pitched scream split the morning quiet. I bolted to my feet. Pilgrim growled deep in his throat. I held his nose, trying to keep him calm while my own knees shook. I scanned the prairie ahead. The grass was still, unmoving. I couldn't see anyone. Then I heard it again.

"Help me! Oh, please, it hurts!"

The unmistakable crack of a pistol silenced the cries. Pilgrim startled and whinnied. He threw his head, and I grabbed hold of his reins. Another gunshot broke through the cold air. I kept my eyes peeled in the direction of the shots, but I couldn't see movement.

Someone called my name. I stepped into Pilgrim's saddle and pulled myself up quickly. "Let's go, Pilgrim!" We raced forward, Pilgrim stretching into a full run across the prairie.

Then I saw something out of the corner of my eye and pulled up sharply, nearly losing my seat. It was Daisy. She was on the ground, her leg caught in a trap. I jumped down and ran to her side.

"Logan! I was looking for you and—" Her voice broke as she grabbed at her leg.

I pinched the release on the trap and slowly dragged it off her bloody foot. She cried out and grabbed my shirt.

"Hush, Daisy," I whispered fiercely, trying to get her to concentrate on my words. "The thieves are just ahead. They're the ones who set these traps." We were within shouting distance of the robbers, but I couldn't see them from where Daisy sat in the grass, lamed by the trap.

Another gunshot rang out. Then I heard Wyatt's voice. "This here is Wyatt Earp! You boys better dough over, or you'll be meetin' your maker today!"

Daisy muffled her cries in my chest as she struggled with the pain. A man called out, "I ain't gonna die for the price of no wagon! The money is buried yonder. Don't shoot!"

"Come on out real slow," Wyatt hollered.

Daisy whispered, "Logan, I came to fetch you. I slipped out on Ginger as soon as it got dark." She closed her eyes to steady herself. Her head seemed too heavy for her shoulders. "It's your pa," she murmured. Then her eyes rolled back, and she collapsed against me.

CHAPTER 19

PILGRIM'S RESCUE

"Daisy!" She was out cold. I ripped my shirt across the bottom and wrapped the cloth tightly around her foot, trying to stop the bleeding. Pilgrim didn't run off, as I gathered Daisy's horse had done. He came when I whistled.

I pulled Daisy's arm over my shoulder and got her to her feet, but I couldn't lift her into the saddle. "Daisy, wake up."

Her head flopped to my shoulder, her hair spilling down. Fear grabbed me. Not far away, Wyatt yelled at the robbers. I looked up at Pilgrim, so tall and steady.

I lowered Daisy to the ground and went to him. "I need your help here, Pilgrim." His ears perked up. "I need you to lay down, boy. Lay down now and help Daisy."

I reached down to his leg and tried to bend it. Not understanding, he picked up his hoof. I shook my head. "No, Pilgrim. Down."

He lowered his hoof and stood steady, looking at me. I knelt in front of him and pulled firmly on his reins. "Down, Pilgrim."

He raised his head back and tried to pull me to my feet. But I pulled harder and bent down to the ground. I reached forward and patted the ground with my free hand. "Down, Pilgrim."

He hesitated, then bent his leg and knelt down. I could tell he was nervous to be in such a compromising position with gunshots going off. But he trusted me. I spoke calmly and pulled tight on his reins. "Good, Pilgrim. All the way down."

The big horse sighed heavily and turned onto his side. I dragged Daisy under her arms and positioned her across the saddle. Pilgrim breathed nervously but didn't move. With one hand steadying Daisy, I slipped my own leg over the saddle. Then I rocked Pilgrim once, twice. Finally understanding, he stepped to his feet, pulling both of us up with him. Daisy moaned.

"Good boy," I said, turning him in the direction of the men, then glanced down at the open trap that snared Daisy. There could be more of them still in the grass. I couldn't take the chance with Pilgrim. I thought about yelling out to Wyatt but decided against it. I didn't want to call attention to us if the robbers were in a desperate situation up there.

I wrapped my arms around Daisy and turned Pilgrim around. I gave him his head and let him go. I didn't look back. I knew it would be hours before we reached Wichita.

Daisy woke only once, trying to hold her own while Pilgrim carried us both. I slowed Pilgrim to a walk, conserving his energy.

"We're going home, Daisy," I said, in my most assuring voice. "Your pa will fix you right up."

Before I could say more, Daisy slumped forward, nearly tossing us both. I called to her. I didn't want to exhaust her, but one thing still bothered me.

It's your pa. I shook the dark thoughts that kept threatening to choke me. We came to a narrow creek, and I bent over Daisy as we threaded our way through the low limbs of the trees. Suddenly, Pilgrim stopped cold. The skin on his neck bristled and twitched and his ears turned back. I knew better than to coax him forward. He was scared. I scanned the ground in front of us for snakes.

It wasn't a snake. Two boys stepped from the trees, their dark faces solemn. The taller of the two raised a hand. They wore buckskin pants and beaded shirts with sleeves. They had moccasins on their feet, and feathers were braided into their long loose hair. My heart pounded furiously. They approached me slowly, careful not to spook Pilgrim.

CHAPTER 20
KIOWA TERRITORY

My mind raced. All I knew about Indians, I'd read in books. I wasn't sure which tribe was which. My rifle was tied down under my saddlebag, completely out of reach.

The taller one had a knife tucked in a pouch and tied around his waist. He seemed to be the leader. Their eyes were bright and took everything in—my rifle, Pilgrim's skittishness, and Daisy's blood-soaked ankle.

I decided to try something. "Please," I began, looking at the older boy. I pointed to Daisy's ankle. "She's hurt. Let us pass."

He crossed his arms across his chest. Maybe he thought I was asking for help. I motioned across the creek and said, "We need to go there."

They looked confused but unafraid. In fact, they seemed fearless and did not respond. Then I remembered something. I steadied Daisy against my right arm and slowly moved my left hand up in the air. I held it up and spoke slowly. "I have something."

They watched like lions ready to pounce as I reached back and carefully slid the small pouch of beads from my bag. I held it out and said, "A trade."

No one moved. Time seemed to stand still until finally the taller boy reached out and snatched the bag from my hand.

He loosened the strings of the pouch and looked inside, emotionless. He pulled the strings again, and I thought he might toss it into the creek. Instead, he started speaking to his friend, their voices low and monotone. I couldn't take my eyes off of them. The younger one gestured to Daisy. He spoke rapidly and kept pointing at her. I tightened my arms around her, ready to ride hard if they tried anything.

Then I noticed he was pointing at her necklace. I tried to remember who made it for her. Was it Kiowa? I couldn't tell if Daisy's necklace was a good thing or not.

Finally, the leader of the two stiffened his back and put his fist against his chest. When I didn't respond, he repeated the gesture, this time smacking his chest so hard I almost grimaced. He motioned for me to cross the creek.

I didn't hesitate. I didn't want to seem too untrusting, but I couldn't take my eyes off them as we crossed. As soon as Pilgrim's hooves dug into the opposite bank, we were off, running again. *Were they there when we passed through yesterday?*

I concentrated on keeping us headed north. My arms cramped up, and my head throbbed from squinting against the bright sun. I shifted in the saddle, trying to adjust my weight to stop the spasm that had taken over my lower back. Daisy's ankle was now dripping

blood, and I imagined a tracker easily following our trail.

My throat was parched, and Pilgrim needed a break. I couldn't allow him a drink back at the creek. Daisy groaned. I had to check her ankle and get a fresh bandage on that wound. The big question was whether or not I could get us back up on Pilgrim.

At the next waterhole, I stopped Pilgrim underneath a nearby cottonwood. Keeping my left foot in the stirrup, I held onto Daisy and pulled my right leg around. I almost lost my balance completely but finally slid Daisy down and gently laid her on the ground.

Pilgrim walked to the water. Loosening Daisy's laces, I eased the shoe from her foot. The metal teeth of the trap had punctured her stockings and bitten into her skin, leaving gaping holes in her ankle and lower shin. Pressure helped slow the bleeding, but her shin had swollen and turned purple as a plum, likely infected.

I wished I had some of the spirits John had swigged last night to clean Daisy's wound. Alcohol was exactly what I needed. Nothing in my saddlebag would help. The best I could do was pour water over it. I went to the creek to fill my canteen and bring Pilgrim back.

When I returned, Daisy's eyes were open. She watched me, a tear rolling down her cheek.

"Nice to have you back," I said with a small smile. "How are you feeling?"

She licked her chapped lips and whispered, "Superior, first-rate, excellent."

I grinned. "Where did you pick that up, I wonder?"

"A cute little girl I know."

"Well, you're a liar anyway." I crouched down beside her.

Daisy wiped her forehead. She looked up at the sky and said, "Your pa took a turn for the worse. When I found out, I came after you. I left Wichita right after you did, thinking I could catch up. But when night came, I got lost."

She looked at me. "I was so scared, Logan. I didn't think I would ever see you again. I thought my daddy would have to—" She broke off and looked back at the sky. "The coyotes kept howling—it seemed like they were getting closer. Finally, I found a place to lie down. I didn't last long there though—too many bugs crawling around." Daisy made a face. "I got back on Ginger. I think I must have fallen asleep, because next thing I knew, I was on the ground and she had taken off. Maybe I was dreaming, but I thought I heard singing. It was dawn, and I went toward the singing, thinking it might be you. That's when this happened." She looked at her ankle.

"For future reference, I can't sing." I offered her a drink from my canteen. "I need to clean your ankle and put another bandage on it. Do you think you can bear it?"

Daisy looked unsure, but she slowly nodded. I tore another strip off my shirt and bandaged her ankle, taking care not to jostle it too much. When I finished, I looked at her to see if she was in pain. She looked at me for a long moment, and I knew what it meant to be thanked without words.

I wanted to ask about Pa, but something in the distance caught my eye—men on horseback heading our way.

I pointed. "I'm sure that's Wyatt's big Appaloosa—looks like there are four of them. No, I see five horses."

Daisy pulled herself up to a sitting position. "Ginger!"

The thieves were tied to their horses and didn't look pleased to be headed back to Wichita. Wyatt and John helped Daisy sit sidesaddle on Ginger, taking care not to bump her foot. John rejected my idea to pour his whiskey on her ankle, although I wasn't sure if it was because he didn't want to hurt her or that he didn't want to waste any. All he said was, "We're close enough to Wichita. I'd rather her pa doctor it up."

We rode together in silence. I held tight to Ginger's lead rope. Wyatt led the group, and John followed behind the prisoners. They weren't much older than me—maybe eighteen. They looked tough and hardened, but Wyatt informed me they were no match with their pistols and gave up easily, pointing out where they had buried the stolen money. He grinned when he described how fast they shoveled that dirt.

CHAPTER 21

HOME TO WICHITA

At last we arrived in Wichita. Wyatt and John turned their horses towards the sheriff's office with the thieves in tow. Daisy and I headed off in the direction of her house.

"Do you think your pa is home?" I asked, trying to keep the conversation on her pa and not mine. A bad feeling had come over me, and I felt hollow.

Daisy shrugged. "I don't know." When we got to her house, I helped her off Ginger. She leaned on me and limped up the front porch steps. There was a light on inside.

"Daisy!" Dr. Kramer swept his daughter up in his arms. "Darling, what have you done?"

Daisy didn't answer; she couldn't. Tears of exhaustion and relief slid down her cheeks.

I spoke for her. "It was a trap, Dr. Kramer. The outlaws set them up all around their camp. Daisy came looking for me and wandered into their snares."

Dr. Kramer's face tightened as he carried his daughter inside. He seemed too choked up for words, so he busied himself with loosening the bandage. Daisy whimpered.

"I should stitch it up," he said. "From the looks of Logan's shirt, he did a good turn by bandaging your ankle."

Dr. Kramer turned to me. "Thank you for bringing my girl home to me." Then a darkness crossed his face. Whatever was troubling him, I didn't want to hear it.

"Logan, your pa's fever spiked, and he had to be put in an ice bath shortly after you took off out of here," Dr. Kramer explained. He turned to Daisy. "Likely, that's why she went after you."

Daisy didn't look at me. Dr. Kramer sighed heavily, his hand on my shoulder as if to brace me. "He's in the back room. He hasn't been conscious since right after you left. Perhaps I should have sent him to the Topeka hospital."

My legs felt like jelly. Pa hadn't been conscious for over 24 hours. I thought back to the message he had put in my pack. Would those be the last words he never said to me?

CHAPTER 22
AN HONEST APOLOGY

Dr. Kramer explained the situation. "I sent your mother home to rest. I also telegraphed her parents in St. Louis. The Coxes are keeping Lizzie."

"It's that grave?"

He looked at me solemnly. "I think you should prepare yourself, Logan. I've done all I can. Now it's up to your pa."

The room seemed to be closing in on me, as if it were getting darker somehow. I wondered if that's the way life would be if Pa died—darker. "May I see him?"

Dr. Kramer took me back into the examining room. Pa was on a bed next to an ice tub. His eyes were closed, his eyelashes darkening the circles under his eyes.

Dr. Kramer drew the curtain that separated the two rooms, leaving me with Pa. As soon as he was gone, I grabbed Pa's hand. His skin was clammy and reminded me of death.

I rested my head on his hand and finally allowed my feelings to overwhelm me. "Pa, wake up. I'm back now. I shouldn't have left, but you wanted me to go. Why did you want me to go?" I sniffed, wiping my face.

"Pa, I got the note you wrote me." I watched his face for any sign that he could hear my words. "I know you've always wanted the best for me. I reckon that's why you brought us here; I just didn't see it right away. I'm sorry." My voice broke. I sobbed long and hard into his hand.

When the tears subsided, I wiped my cheeks. "Looks like you could use a fresh cloth." I took the rag to the water basin and wrung it out in cool water. When I laid it back across Pa's forehead, I glanced at the small bedside table. Daisy's fossil and our family picture were right where I could see them. The fossil was Daisy's way of telling Pa that we all leave part of ourselves behind. She hadn't needed words to tell him.

I picked up the picture and stared at Pa. He looked so proud, his shoulders back and his chin out. Then I saw his hand on my shoulder. I remembered that moment. I'd felt like he was doing it for show. *I always questioned you.*

I sat at the foot of his bed, staring at the picture, imagining what it would look like without Pa in it. Leaning my head back, I closed my eyes, exhausted. Crawling into my own bed sounded good, but I was his only son. My place was here.

I lit the kerosene lamp and drew my notes from my pocket. After organizing my thoughts, I began to write the story that kept me from my father's bedside, the story of my adventure with Wyatt Earp. My father knew how important this would be. I had a duty to him to write this story.

The words fell into place, one after another, pouring onto the page as if already written in my head, just waiting to be released. When I finished, I laid the papers on Pa's nightstand and collapsed into the chair beside him.

Dr. Kramer shook me awake. The morning sunlight crossed the floor and crept halfway up the wall.

"Logan, his fever broke." Dr. Kramer still looked concerned.

"Did he wake up?"

Dr. Kramer shook his head slowly. "No." He listened to Pa's breathing and then turned toward the curtain that separated the two rooms. "There's something out here I think you'll like to see." I must have looked confused because he said, "Go ahead, your family is waiting."

I opened the curtain and gasped.

"Well, that's a fine how-do-you-do!" Gramps exclaimed. Gram opened her arms wide, and I rushed into them.

"Look how you've grown!" Gramps thundered. "What do they feed younguns in Wichita?"

I smiled wanly. Gram squeezed my hand, knowing I wasn't in a jovial mood.

Mama hugged me hard and then looked at my face, searching for something.

Dr. Kramer spoke up. "I can report that his fever is down, Mable."

Mama nodded thankfully. Gramps put his hand on Mama's shoulder and said, "Now see, Pearl, everything will be fine." He turned to Dr. Kramer and added, "Won't it, Doc?"

Dr. Kramer looked reluctant to speak. He opened his mouth as if to say something, but he must have thought better of it, because he snapped it shut and nodded. Finally, he said, "He's certainly a fighter."

I noticed Daisy sitting on the couch, her wounded leg propped up on a stack of pillows. She grinned.

"Your grandparents are exactly as you described," she said, holding her hand out to Gram, who took it and patted Daisy affectionately.

"Don't believe a word of it!" Gramps cautioned.

Dr. Kramer spoke up. "I need to run a few errands this morning. I would appreciate one of you staying with our patient."

We all stayed. We took turns sitting with Pa. Gram helped Reba make sandwiches in the kitchen. Mrs. Cox dropped Lizzie off, and Gramps kept Daisy and her busy with his stories.

Mama sat on the sofa, quiet. I sat beside her. "Dr. Kramer's right, Ma—Pa's a fighter."

Mama nodded. She wiped away a tear and looked down at her lap. In a soft voice she said, "I'm so worried. There's no money to pay Dr. Kramer. I don't know how we'll manage."

Nothing I could say would make her words less true. We weren't prepared for Pa to be ill. My thoughts went back to Ethan's family. Would we also be out in the street? Would we give up and move back to St. Louis? It was funny, but I wanted to stay in Wichita.

I was by Pa's bedside when he woke up. His eyes fluttered a few times before he fixed his gaze on me. He tried to speak, but nothing came out. I lifted his head and put a glass of water to his lips. His hand moved slowly up to mine. He grabbed my wrist and held it.

"I should get Mama." I turned to leave.

"Wait." He didn't release my wrist. "Logan. I should have done more."

"Pa, don't."

He shook his head to silence me. "You're my son. I want you to know." He stared at me. "I love you, Logan."

I was not ashamed of my tears. "I love you too, Pa."

He wrapped his arms around me and didn't let go, even when Mama came into the room, exclaiming when she saw him awake.

The room filled with people. Gramps held Lizzie in his arms. Gram helped Daisy hobble in, and soon everyone was chattering away, telling Pa how Mama's parents took the train as soon as they heard of his illness, telling what had happened to Daisy's leg and how the thieves had been captured.

Then Dr. Kramer drew back the curtain. "What a sight for sore eyes!" He entered the room. I was surprised to see Mr. Murdock and Wyatt Earp behind him.

Mr. Murdock spoke first. "Logan, you've had quite the week. I wanted to be the first to tell you that Mr. Whitney is setting the type for your story to run in this week's paper. You have the lead story!"

I turned to look at Pa's bedside table, where I left my writing from last night. It wasn't there. Dr. Kramer cleared his throat. "I hope you don't mind, son. I thought it best to get such a fine story to the paper as quickly as possible."

Wyatt stepped forward. "The two men you helped us track down are in jail. There was a reward for the return of the stolen money from the Tisdale stage. The reward was $60. If your math is as good as your writing, I think you'll agree that your part is $20." He held out two gold coins.

I just stared. Here was the money it would take to support our family so Pa could recover. The entire room seemed to be waiting for me to do something.

Wyatt stepped forward and shoved the money into my hand. "Take it. You're a born reporter." He tipped his hat to Gram and Mama.

Pa spoke next, his voice weak, but even. "Mr. Murdock, be sure to bring me that paper so I can read my son's first lead story."

I looked at Pa. His face told me everything. He was proud of me. I knew then that we were going to be amazing, fantastic, wonderful! Our new life was only just beginning.

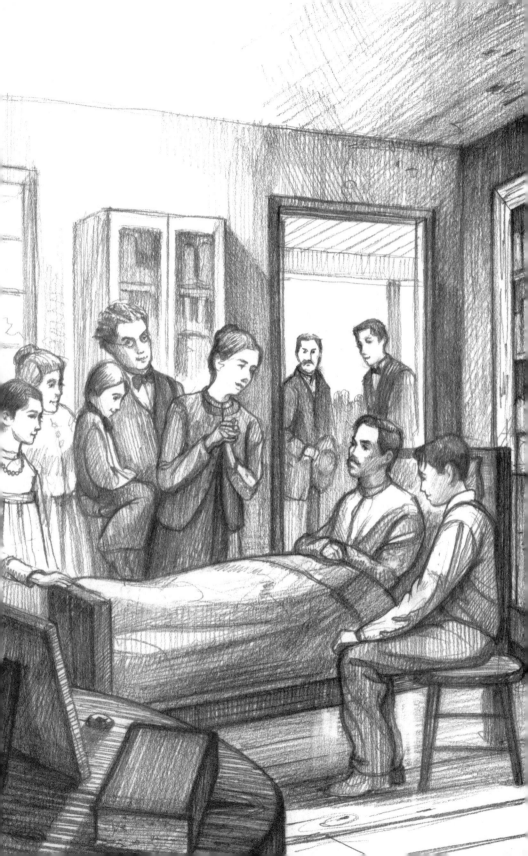